HE ONLY WANTED A MEAL

Quince was just pulling the chair out from the table when, out of the corner of his eye, he saw someone moving toward him with a pistol in his hand. Though he didn't know his assailant's name, he recognized him as one of Deekus Tombs' gang.

Quince wondered, briefly, if the whole gang was here and if he might be surrounded. But there was no time to dwell on that, because the man coming toward him was already bringing his pistol to bear. Quince slipped his own pistol out of his holster and suddenly the room shattered with the roar of two guns exploding. . . .

Ralph Compton's
Runaway Stage

A Novel by Robert Vaughan

A SIGNET BOOK

SIGNET
Published by New American Library, a division of
Penguin Putnam Inc., 375 Hudson Street,
New York, New York 10014, U.S.A.
Penguin Books Ltd, 80 Strand,
London WC2R 0RL, England
Penguin Books Australia Ltd, Ringwood,
Victoria, Australia
Penguin Books Canada Ltd, 10 Alcorn Avenue,
Toronto, Ontario, Canada M4V 3B2
Penguin Books (N.Z.) Ltd, 182–190 Wairau Road,
Auckland 10, New Zealand

Penguin Books Ltd, Registered Offices:
Harmondsworth, Middlesex, England

First published by Signet, an imprint of New American Library,
a division of Penguin Putnam Inc.

First Printing, January 2002
10 9 8 7 6 5 4 3 2 1

PUBLISHER'S NOTE
This is a work of fiction. Names, characters, places, and incidents either
are the product of the author's imagination or are used fictitiously,
and any resemblance to actual persons, living or dead, business
establishments, events, or locales is entirely coincidental.

Chapter One

The prison guard held his lantern up to the barred window and, with the reflector, cast a beam of light into the shadowed cell. He played the light through the dark until it fell upon the bunk. There, Quince Fremont was lying on his back with his hands folded behind his head. His eyes were open.

"How come you still awake?" the guard asked.

"I can't sleep," Quince replied.

The guard snorted. "That's the problem with prison nowadays. They don't work you cons hard enough to make you tired. What with all the soft living and good food, hell, we'll soon have folks trying to break into prison."

"That's true, Jack," Quince said to the guard. "Why, I get letters from people all the time, asking if they can trade places with me."

"How long you been here, Fremont?"

"Six months."

"Six months, huh? Six months and you're still a smart ass," the guard said. "But you're going to be here a long time, and I guarantee you, you won't be such a smart ass when you leave. I'll break you, you can count on that."

"You have a real winning personality, Jack. Has anyone ever told you that?" Quince asked.

The guard pulled the light down and, once more, the cell was plunged into darkness. Quince lay perfectly still on his bunk, as he listened to the receding clomp of the guard's footsteps, and the echoing rattle of cell doors being checked.

When he was certain the guard was gone, he hopped out of bed, then reached down into his burlap bag. From the bag he extracted what looked like a gourd. A closer examination, however, showed the gourd to be a work of art. Hair and eyebrows, made from real hair, helped create the illusion of a man's face. Quince placed the gourd on his small, thin pillow, then draped the blanket in such a way as to make it appear as if a man was sleeping in the bunk.

With the dummy in place, Quince pulled the cap off the hollow frame of his bedstand and started pulling on the string that hung down inside. Attached to the other end of the string was the key he had been working on for the last several days.

The keyhole on the door to his cell had a center probe, which meant that the key shaft had to be hollow. Quince managed that by using the legbone of a rabbit, with all the marrow scraped out. It took him several tries to get the interior diameter just right. He established the diameter by rolling paper into a tight cylinder, then sticking his arm through the cell door window, and pushing the paper into the keyhole. The probe in the keyhole depressed the paper in such a way that would allow him to estimate the probe's dimensions. Now he had a hollowed piece of bone that was of the proper size and bore to work effectively as a key shaft.

He located the settings of the tumblers by cutting several narrow slits in a tin can, then sticking the tin can into the keyhole and turning it. The tumblers displaced the appropriate fingers on the pliable tin, thus providing Quince with a template. Now all he had to do was lay that template alongside the hollow bone shaft, and put the key flanges in the appropriate place. These he made from bits of metal salvaged from an old saw. It took several tries, modifications, and retries before the key was finally ready for use. Then, once the key was ready, he had to choose the right time to make his escape.

Tonight was the right time.

Quince stepped up to the cell door, stuck his arm through the window, inserted the key carefully, then turned. He felt some pressure on the key and hesitated. It wouldn't do to break the key off in the lock now.

Taking a deep breath, Quince put a little more pressure into his effort, then was rewarded with a satisfying click as his sawtooth flanges tripped the tumblers in the lock. He turned the key all the way, then quietly pushed the door open. Cautiously, he stuck his head out and looked up and down the long hallway. The guard who had checked on him a moment earlier was gone now.

Quince closed the door and locked it behind him, then he looked through the window back into his cell. The dummy was doing its job. From this angle, and in this reduced light, it looked exactly as if he were still in bed.

Dropping to his hands and knees to lessen the chances of his being seen in silhouette, Quince crawled quickly down the hallway until he reached the end. There, as soon as he rounded the corner, he was able to stand and move, for it was unlikely that he would be spotted in this area.

At the end of this corridor was a barred window. At first glance, it looked formidable, but Quince knew its weakness. While working on a painting detail earlier, he saw that the anchoring bolts were so loose that they could easily be pulled from the wall. Quince had painted over the bolts to cover up their weakness.

Now, he pulled on the bars and they easily came away from the wall. Next he opened the window, climbed through, reset the bars behind him, then dropped down onto the ground.

Moving swiftly through the dark, he hurried to the warden's house. It wasn't by accident that he had chosen tonight to escape. This was Friday night, and every Friday night three of the warden's closest friends would come in from town to play cards. They always arrived together, riding in the doctor's buckboard. They would play cards with the warden, have a couple of drinks, then at precisely ten o'clock, they would leave.

They always left the team attached to the buckboard, and Quince saw the horses, standing silently in the darkness. Moving quietly, Quince stepped from the shadow of the warden's house and out to the hitching rail. There, he shushed the horses, then crawled under the buckboard to put the next part of his plan into operation. Quince was going to use the buckboard as his means of getting through the front gate. To this end, he fastened loops of rope to the underside of the wagon, then, testing it, he stuck his feet and hands through the ropes. This enabled him to lift himself up and press right against the bottom, essentially tying himself to the bottom of the buckboard. Lowering himself back down, he stepped over into nearby hedgerow to lessen his chances of being seen. There, he would wait until the poker game broke up.

With everything done now, except playing the waiting game, Quince looked back toward the big, dimly lit block house from which he had just come. So far there had been no alarm given, which indicated that his dummy had fooled the watch guard.

Half an hour later, the front door to the warden's house opened and a wedge of orange lantern light spilled out onto the front porch. Laughing, three men came outside, accompanied by the warden.

"Warden, I thank you for your, uh, donation tonight," one of the men said, and the others chuckled.

"Yes, well, the cards might have run well for you tonight, Sheriff, but I'll get even with you next week," the warden replied.

"Even? Hell, Warden, you could lose for the next six months and still be ahead," one of the others said.

"Of course I'm way ahead. Why else do you think I want you fellas to come out and play every week?" the warden replied.

As they were saying their good-byes, Quince moved out of the shadows and slipped under the buckboard. Sticking his feet through the rope loops he had tied in place, he grabbed the other two loops then secured himself.

A moment later, the wagon started toward the front gate. As they passed the kennel, the dogs started barking.

"What's got the dogs all upset, do you suppose?" one of the men asked.

"Ah, you know how they are. The least little thing can set them off."

The dogs barked louder and louder, becoming more agitated.

"Well, hurry it up, those animals are some mean-looking sons of bitches," one of the men said.

"They sure are. Wouldn't you hate to be an escaped prisoner with those things after you?"

One of the dogs managed to leap over the kennel fence and came rushing toward the wagon, growling viciously, his fangs bared. He darted under the wagon and took a nip of Quince's leg. Quince felt the painful tear of his flesh being ripped open, but he gritted his teeth and remained quiet.

"Get the hell out of there!" one of the men in the wagon said. He banged against the side of the wagon with his whip.

"What's going on?" one of the guards asked as the wagon stopped at the gate.

"What's going on? I'll tell you what's going on. Your damn dogs have gone crazy," the sheriff answered. "Call him off."

The guard yelled at the dog, who crouched,

his head low as he continued to snarl. Finally one of the dog handlers arrived.

"What's got into him?" the guard asked.

The handler shrugged his shoulders. "Who knows?" he answered. "Sometimes they get like that."

"Well, open the gate, man," the wagon driver asked. "I'd like to get out of here before he takes it in his mind to attack us."

The guard nodded at someone who was up on the wall, and the gate, assisted by counter-weights, opened for the wagon. The driver snapped his reins and the team moved forward through the night.

Quince hung on beneath the wagon until his feet and hands were numb. Then, when he was sure he was far enough away not to be seen in the darkness, he dropped to the ground. The wagon passed over him, then continued on its way. Quince lay in the dirt for a long moment, unable to move because of the loss of circulation. Finally, and painfully, his circulation returned and with a prickly feeling in his hands and feet, he was able to get up and move out of the road.

He ran through the rest of the night, not stopping until the sun came up the next morning. From the top of a hill, he saw a small building he recognized at once as a line-shack. A small wisp of smoke curling from the chimney told him that the line-shack was occupied.

Half an hour later, a man came out of the little house, still eating a biscuit. Quince watched as he saddled his horse, then rode off to tend to the day's chores.

Slowly, Quince moved down the hill to the shack, then he sneaked up to look through the window. As he had hoped, it was empty.

Inside proved to be a bonanza for him. He made a meal of biscuits, beans, and bacon. He also found a change of clothes, a pistol belt complete with a .44 Colt, and $14.25 in an empty coffee can.

Fed, dressed, armed, and funded, Quince was about to leave, but just as he started out the front door, he hesitated. The fact that he was an innocent man, wrongly imprisoned, gave him all the moral justification he needed for doing what he was doing. Logically, this was survival, not burglary.

And yet, though he could vindicate his actions, he couldn't help but think of the man he was stealing from. To the poor cowboy who was manning this line-shack, fourteen dollars represented a month's wages. Add the pistol and clothes and it might be two months' wages.

A packet of letters not only told Quince that the man could read . . . it also told him his name. Against his better judgment, but in compliance with his conscience, Quince found a paper and pencil and left a note.

Dear Mr. Dan Davis,

I'm sorry I had to take your duds and money but I am in desperate need. I'm not stealing, I'm buying your clothes and gun, and borrowing your money. I know your name, and promise to send you $100 as soon as I can.

Quince didn't sign the note.

Quince Fremont's problems had begun less than a year earlier, when a man named Deekus Tombs held up a bank in Theresa, Wyoming.

It was an early afternoon in the middle of May and Theresa was busy. Wagons were parked in front of all the stores, horses were tied at the hitching rails, and men and women hurried up and down the board sidewalks.

Onto this scene of commercial activity rode seven men. The town was so busy that the men barely attracted attention, though a few of the townsmen did glance at the leader, a medium-sized man with a pockmarked face and a drooping left eyelid. Deekus Tombs and his fellow riders surveyed the town carefully, studying the rooflines of the false-fronted buildings, looking into the open doorways and peering down the alleyways. These men were wanted all over the West, and they entered every town the same way, knowing that at any given time they might well ride into an ambush of lawmen, vigilantes, or just good citizens.

"Sure seems like a busy place," Felton Pogue said, scratching his dark, stubbly beard.

"Yeah, well, maybe that's good," his brother Billy replied, riding beside him. "The more people in the street, the easier it'll be for us to get away."

"There! There's the bank right down there on the corner, just like I said," Jim Silver said, pointing out the building.

"Quit pointin'," Deekus ordered. "You want folks to start gettin' suspicious?"

"I don't see how just pointin' at the bank is goin' to make anyone suspicious."

"That's 'cause you ain't got the sense God give a goose," Felton said. "Just shut up and pay attention to what Deekus tells you."

"Felton I swear, one of these days . . ." Silver said, without finishing the threat.

"One of these days what?" Billy Pogue asked.

"Wasn't talkin' to you, I was talkin' to your brother."

"You talk to one of us, you talk to both of us," Billy said.

"Shut up, all of you," Deekus ordered. "We

got some business to take care of. We can't be fightin' amongst ourselves."

"Hey, Deekus, how much money you reckon's in that bank?" Hawk Peters asked.

"I don't know," Deekus answered. "Maybe a couple of thousand dollars. It don't really make no difference. A bank's a bank, and money is money."

"How we goin' to do this? We just goin' to ride right in and hit it, or what?"

"Not so fast," Deekus answered. He pointed to a small restaurant across the street. "What say we get us somethin' to eat first? From there we can sort of keep an eye on things for a while."

"Yeah, that's a good idea," Felton said, scratching his beard.

"Felton, anytime we eat, you figure it's a good idea," his brother quipped, tugging on his light brown mustache. The others laughed.

"Well, I tell you, Billy, there ain't too many of us seen you turn down a meal," Hawk Peters said.

The men dismounted in front of the restaurant, then went inside and ordered ham, eggs, biscuits, and fried potatoes. Their food came, and to anyone watching who had not seen their faces on wanted posters, they appeared merely to be seven friends lingering over a meal for some friendly conversation.

Shortly after two o'clock, the seven men left the restaurant. The two Pogue brothers rode to the north end of town, Hawk Peters and Jim Silver went to the south, while Deekus, Angus Wilson, and Clint Prescott casually walked their horses across the street and hitched them directly in front of the bank. For a few minutes they stood at the door, then, suddenly, the Pogue boys, Hawk, and Jim Silver came riding from either end of the town at a full gallop, shooting and whooping loudly, and scattering the terrified bystanders. With the citizens' attention diverted from the bank, Deekus, Wilson, and Prescott rushed inside.

"Put your hands up!" Deekus shouted gruffly the moment they stepped through the door.

The two women customers screamed, while one male customer, Ned O'Leary, shouted out in anger, only to be clubbed down by the butt of Wilson's pistol.

"Ever'one keep quiet," Prescott said. "We'll do all the talkin'. You—get a couple of bags and start fillin' them with cash."

With shaking hands, the teller began scooping money out of the open bank drawers and dropping it into a couple of cloth bags.

"Now let's get some real money. You," Deekus said to the bank teller who was standing nearest the vault, "start emptyin' out that safe."

The middle-aged banker put his hand on the

door, then, to Deekus's surprise, he abruptly slammed it shut.

"That was a stupid thing to do. You're just gonna have to open it again," Deekus said.

With a smug smile, the banker shook his head. "Not till eight o'clock tomorrow morning."

"What do you mean?"

"It's a time lock. It's impossible for anyone to open it before eight tomorrow. So, you're just going to have to find another bank to rob, Mr. Tombs."

"Damn you!" Deekus growled. Without a moment's hesitation, he shot the banker in the chest.

Eyes growing wide, the banker gasped, fell against the front of the vault, then slid down to a sitting position, leaving a swath of blood on the vault door from his exit wound. He took two or three gasping breaths, then died.

"The cash drawers empty?" Deekus called.

"Yes," Prescott answered.

"Then let's get the hell out of here."

The bank president, who had crept out the back door of his office when the robbery began, now darted up between two buildings until he was in the middle of main street. There, he began shouting, "The bank is being robbed! The bank is being robbed!"

The townspeople suddenly recognized the great show of gunplay for the ruse it was and began arming themselves. Ducking behind barrels and crouching in windows, men started firing at the four mounted outlaws. The outlaws quit firing into the air and began shooting back.

Felton Pogue shot one man as he rose up from behind a crate to get off a shot from his rifle. The man screamed and clutched his shoulder, then fell.

The outlaws jerked their horses about, making them prance so as to be more difficult targets. They waited anxiously for their cohorts to emerge from the bank, firing off shot after shot as they kept the townspeople busy.

Inside the bank, Ned O'Leary, the customer Wilson had clubbed to the floor regained consciousness. O'Leary normally shied away from any trouble. He had a wife and a small daughter to take care of, and their welfare was always his primary concern. O'Leary owned a hotel and a restaurant in Antelope Springs, a town near Theresa. He had opened an account at the larger bank in Theresa to take advantage of a better loan interest rate, and now found that his life savings was about to be snatched away by these desperadoes. The thought of these outlaws jeopardizing the future of his family made the normally gentle O'Leary irate. Seeing what was going on, he managed to pull his gun.

"Hold it right there!" he shouted.

Wilson turned toward O'Leary and fired, but

missed. O'Leary gamely fired back. Wilson grabbed his chest, then went down.

"You son of a bitch!" Deekus shouted. He shot Ned O'Leary in the heart, then he and Prescott rushed out the front door of the bank, each one of them holding a money sack stuffed with the bills taken from the cash drawers. Most of the bank's money was still behind them, untouched, on the shelves of the time-locked vault. When the two robbers stepped outside the bank, they were stopped in their tracks by the sight of the battle taking place just down the street.

"What the hell?" Deekus shouted. "My God, what's going on here? We're in a full-scale war!"

Seeing Deekus and Prescott come out, the citizens of the community swarmed toward the bank.

"Hold it! You ain't goin' nowhere!" a middle-aged townsman called as he fired his pistol. The bullet missed Deekus and punched through the front window of the bank. Another man fired a shot and his bullet clipped Deekus's hat.

"Let's go, let's go!" Deekus yelled to his men.

"Where's Wilson?" Billy shouted.

"He's dead. Let's ride!"

From the restaurant in which the men had eaten a few minutes earlier, a citizen, food stains spattered on the front of his shirt, appeared with a shotgun. He let go a blast, but the gun was loaded with light bird shot, and his pellets merely peppered the outlaws without penetrating their skin. Another man with a shotgun fired, and the front window of the bank came crashing down.

A man killed Billy Pogue's horse, and Hawk yelled at Felton, "Your brother's been dismounted!"

Seeing Billy standing in the street, Felton dashed toward one of the hitching rails. Several horses had been left tied by their owners all along the street. Spooked by all the gunfire, they were rearing and pulling against their restraints. Felton tried for one, but it got away as soon as he untied it. So did the second one. Felton managed to grab the reins of the third animal.

At that moment, the horse's owner started forward in protest, shouting, "That's my horse!"

"It's my brother's horse now," Felton retorted, shooting the man between the eyes from point-blank range.

With all the outlaws mounted, they galloped toward the south end of town. Seeing them come that way, several men rolled a wagon out into the middle of the dusty street and tipped it over, creating a barricade. Several of the townsmen gathered around the wagon, with rifles held at the ready.

"What do we do now, Deekus?" Hawk Peters asked.

"This way!" Deekus shouted back, and he

reined his mount around, spinning it toward the large plate-glass window fronting a dressmaking shop. He urged his horse forward, and the animal leapt through the window, shattering the glass with an enormous crashing sound, clearing the way for the other four horses that followed close behind.

There were a number of women in the shop, including one being fitted for a new dress. Covering her half-naked, corseted body with her arms, she and the other ladies screamed in terror as they made a mad dash to get out of the way. The horses clattered and skidded across the wooden floor, then ran through the back door and into an open field behind the store. It was a brilliant move on the part of the outlaws, for none of the townspeople were yet mounted, and by the time they managed to reach their horses and come around the edge of town, the bank robbers had completely disappeared into the timbered hills.

Returning to Theresa, the stunned citizens of the town began to count their dead. There were two in the bank—Emil Dumey, the brave banker who had slammed the door shut on the vault, and Ned O'Leary. Out in the street, three men and a young boy had been killed, the deputy sheriff among them.

Chapter Two

Quince Fremont and his older brother were building a ranch and worked hard to fulfill the dream they shared. They had just come through a bad winter, and cattle losses to weather, wolves, and rustlers were so high that there was a question as to whether or not they could keep the ranch. In order to help out, Quince took a job with the Wyoming Coach and Express Company, working as a shotgun guard. That earned enough to keep them going, but not enough to recoup what they had lost during the winter.

Desperate, they applied at the bank for an extension on their loan, but the request had been turned down. They had to have five thousand dollars within two more days or they would lose the ranch.

Then Cole Fremont approached his brother with an idea. Suppose they leased their land for a period of five years to one of the big Eastern cattle combines? The lease money would pay off the loan. They would sell what was left of their herd to the combine and, at the end of five years, they could start all over again with a new herd on land that they owned free and clear.

Quince didn't much like the idea of letting someone else run cattle on their land, but he had to admit that this was probably the only option open to them. Thus agreed, they started into town to send a few telegrams and make all the arrangements.

They were about four miles outside of town when Quince's horse threw a shoe and the two men had to stop.

"I told you day before yesterday that that shoe looked loose," Cole scolded. "Some rancher you are, little brother. You can't even keep your horse shod."

"Rancher? Who said I was a rancher? I'm a shotgun guard," Quince replied.

"Yes, and that's all you'll ever be if we can't save our ranch," Cole said. He swung down from his horse. "I'd better fix that shoe. I've got some tools in my saddlebag."

Cole had just lifted the left foreleg of Quince's horse to look at the foot when six men came riding hard toward them.

"Wonder what their big hurry is?" Quince asked.

Cole looked toward them with only a passing

interest. His biggest concern was the shoe. "Who knows?" he said.

The horses made an obvious turn so that they were now riding toward them.

"Cole, they're coming right at us," Quince said, uneasily.

"They ain't Indians are they?"

"No."

"Then don't worry 'bout it. Get the file for me, will you?"

Still keeping a wary eye on the approaching riders, Quince took the file from the saddlebag, then handed it to Cole.

The riders came right up to them, then reined to an abrupt halt.

"Howdy," Cole said, looking up from the horse's hoof.

"Havin' some trouble?" one of the riders—a man with a long, pockmarked face and a drooping eyelid—asked, swinging down from his horse. The other five riders dismounted as well.

There was something peculiar about the riders, about the way they stared at Quince and Cole with hard eyes, and how they let one man do all the talking. Two of the riders were wearing identical plaid shirts, and as Quince looked at them more closely, they looked enough alike that he realized that they must be brothers.

"Oh, nothing we can't handle," Cole answered. He squinted at the men. "I don't believe I ever met any of you gents," he said. "Just come into the territory?"

"Yeah, we're lookin' for work," the man with the drooping eyelid said.

Cole shrugged. "Don't know as you'll have too much luck there. Spring roundup's over, so none of the ranches are hirin'. Quince, hand me the spare shoe, would you?"

"All right," Quince said. Quince turned his attention to the saddlebag, when suddenly, he heard his brother call out in an alarmed voice.

"What the hell are you doing, mister?"

Quince whirled back around, just as one of the riders slammed the butt of his pistol down on his head. At the same time he felt a sharp stab of pain, and heard a loud popping noise. He couldn't be sure what it was, however, because at that moment, everything went black.

"Get up," someone ordered.

Opening his eyes, Quince found that he was lying facedown in the dirt. He had no idea where he was or why he was lying on the ground, though he sensed that there were several people standing around looking down at him.

Quince tried to get up, but everything started spinning so badly that he nearly passed out again. He was conscious of a terrible pain on the top of his head, and when he reached up and touched the spot gingerly, his fingers came away sticky with blood. Holding his fingers in front of his eyes, he stared at them in surprise.

"What happened?" he asked, his tongue thick as though he had been drinking too much.

"I'll tell you what happened, mister. Looks to me like there was a fallin' out among thieves," a gruff voice said. "The other boys turned on you two, didn't they? They took the money with them."

Shaking his head slowly, trying to make sense of things, Quince hesitated.

"That's right, ain't it?"

"I don't know what you're talking about," Quince said. "Where's my brother? Where's Cole?"

"Lyin' ain't goin' to do you no good," the man said. "You're the one we want, all right. And just 'cause you wound up without any of the money, it don't make you no less guilty. You're goin' to hang, fella. Your brother would hang, too, if your friends hadn't already killed him. Now, you goin' to get up, or am I goin' to have to tie a rope 'round your feet and drag you all the way back into town?"

"Killed him? Cole is dead?" Quince asked. Looking around, he saw Cole's body. "Cole!" he shouted. He tried to get up to go toward his brother's corpse, but he was shoved back down.

"You just stay there. Don't move till I tell you."

"Who are you?" Quince asked. He had been right in sensing that there were several people around him. In addition to the one who was obviously in charge—a burly man of about forty-five with a deeply lined face—there were six more men glaring at him and brandishing an arsenal of weapons ranging from revolvers to rifles to shotguns . . . all of which were pointing at him.

"The name is Bowie Cade. I'm the sheriff from Theresa," the burly man answered, holding open his jacket to expose the tin star pinned to his shirt. "And these here men are my deputies. I reckon you and your friends figured you could rob our bank, but you got yourselves another thing comin'. Allright, now you can get up."

Quince got up, then went quickly over to Cole. This time, no one tried to stop him.

"Cole!" he cried out in an agonized voice, kneeling beside him and feeling his chest for any sign of life.

"Is that his name? Cole?"

"Yes. Cole Fremont. He's my brother. I'm Quince Fremont." He noticed then, that Cole was wearing a different shirt, one checked with a plaid pattern . . . and, as he looked at himself, Quince realized that he, too, was wearing a plaid shirt. The same two shirts he saw earlier on the two men he had surmised were brothers. "What the hell?" Quince asked, holding out his arm and staring at the shirt. "How did this happen?"

"I told you how it happened," the sheriff said. "You boys got into a little fight, and they lit out on you."

Quince had been asking about the shirt, but the sheriff misunderstood.

"Mister, I'm arrestin' you for the murder and bank robbin' you, your brother, and the others done down in Theresa," Cade said.

One of the other riders grabbed Quince roughly, twisted his hands behind his back, then shackled them together.

"Help him on his horse," Sheriff Cade ordered. "And pick up them empty bank bags. Like as not, we'll be needin' 'em, as evidence."

"Sheriff Cade, you're making a big mistake," Quince said as he was put roughly onto his horse. My brother and I didn't hold up any bank in Theresa. Neither one of us have ever been there."

"You want to explain these empty bank bags here?" Cade asked, holding one of them out for Quince to examine. Clearly printed on the side of the bag was a stencil that read BANK OF THERESA.

"They must've been left here by the men who

25

jumped us. They're the ones you are looking for."

"Jumped, you say?"

"Yes, they knocked me out . . . they must've killed my brother."

"You got witnesses to that?"

"Well, no," Quince said. "Certainly none who would testify, as they would be testifying against themselves."

"Too bad, Fremont. 'Cause I do have witnesses. At least half a dozen of 'em. And they'll ever'one of 'em swear they seen you and your brother ridin' out of town with Deekus Tombs."

Quince's eyes widened with surprise as he suddenly realized who the six riders were. "Deekus Tombs? Well, I'll be damned. That's who it was." Shaking his head angrily, the young rancher set his jaw firmly. "But we weren't with Deekus Tombs. Neither one of us had ever laid eyes on him till he and his men rode up on us, today. Your witnesses are wrong, Sheriff. They are either mistaken, or they are lying."

"Mister, *I am* one of them witnesses," Cade said. "And I don't cotton to being called no liar. So, don't you go tellin' me what I did and what I did not see." He pointed at Quince's chest, adding, "I remember them plaid shirts you and your brother was wearing as if there was a picture of 'em drawn on my eyeballs."

"This isn't my shirt," Quince said. He pointed to Cole's body. "And that isn't the shirt he was wearing when we left our ranch this morning."

Squeezing his eyes shut, then opening them, as if somehow that would bring things into focus, Quince managed to reconstruct a picture of what had happened. It would appear that Deekus Tombs had used Quince and his brother to buy some time from the posse that had given chase after the bank robbery. They had knocked out Quince, killed Cole, then changed shirts with them. To make the frame-up even more believable, they left a couple of empty bank bags nearby.

"You've got the wrong man," Quince insisted. "You are making a huge mistake."

"No, friend," the lawman responded. "The only ones who made any mistakes around here were you and your brother. And you boys made three of 'em." Ticking them off on his fingers, he enumerated: "Your first mistake was pickin' a bank in my town to rob. Your second was trustin' a man like Deekus Tombs, and your third was gettin' yourself caught. Now, let's go."

"What about my brother? You aren't just going to leave him here?"

"I'll send word to the undertaker back in Theresa to come out and get him." Smirking, he added, "Don't worry, he ain't goin' nowhere."

* * *

Quince had not even been allowed to attend his brother's burial. At the time of the funeral, the young rancher was attending his own trial. Although the town sheriff came down from Antelope Springs to testify on Quince's behalf, pointing out that neither he nor Cole had ever given him a lick of trouble, it wasn't enough. The judge sentenced Quince to twenty years of hard labor. But the court had its timetable and Quince had his. By biding his time and picking the best opportunity to escape, Quince managed to cut his sentence down to "time served."

Traveling by night so as to avoid any posse that might be out looking for him, Quince saw the glow of a campfire and cautiously approached. Expecting to find some cowboys in the middle of a roundup bedded down for the night, he moved close enough to be able to see and hear what was going on. He was surprised to discover that it wasn't cowboys at all. And he was downright shocked to see who was hunkered around the licking flares of the campfire: It was Deekus Tombs and his gang. They were discussing their last robbery and planning their next.

There had been a time during his first few months in prison when Quince had been so filled with rage, all he could think of was avenging his brother's death. But now, seeing Deekus, he had the sudden urge to bring him in, so that he might somehow prove his own innocence. Quince knew that he would have to do that to truly be free, for even if he went to Texas, or California, or back East, he would still be a wanted man. Just how he was supposed to accomplish rounding up the gang, however, he had no idea.

"Boys, it's the sweetest deal we ever come across," he heard Deekus saying. "One hundred thousand dollars, all in cash . . . just waitin' for us."

Quince moved a little closer for a better look and to hear more of what they were discussing. As he did, his foot dislodged a large rock, and sent it clattering loudly.

"What the hell was that?" Deekus yelled, his pan of beans flying as he stood up quickly, his gun in his hand in an instant. "Hawk, douse them flames," he ordered. Coffee was immediately thrown on the fire, and it sizzled and smoked as it went out.

Fearing discovery, Quince started to scramble over the boulder-strewn ground in an attempt to get away.

"There! I saw something!" someone shouted, and his voice was followed almost immediately by a shot.

The others began to fire as well, the flames from their gun muzzles lighting up the dark like

29

flashes of summer lightning. Bullets passed so close to Quince's ear that he could feel the sharp puff of air at their passing.

Using the muzzle flashes as targets, Quince fired back. He heard a yelp of pain.

"After him!" one of the bandits yelled. "The son of a bitch got Billy!"

Another bullet careened off a rock by Quince's feet, sending chips of stone flying in the air, one of them slamming painfully against his leg. He was thankful for the thick, sturdy denim cloth that protected his skin; otherwise the chip would have penetrated as if it were a slug.

Quince grew panicked. He could tell by the gang's voices, which were getting steadily and increasingly louder, that the outlaws were drawing closer, keeping up their barrage of lead as they approached.

Suddenly the ground gave way in front of him as he ran over the edge of the cliff. Involuntarily, he let out a yell as he fell.

"We got him!" someone yelled.

"We didn't get him. He fell over the cliff."

"Who was he? Did you see him, Felton?" Deekus asked.

"Yeah, I seen him," Felton said. "It was that fella we set up for the robbery we done a ways back in Theresa."

"Who? Fremont? That was Fremont shooting at us?"

"That's who it was, all right," Felton said.

"Can't be. He's in jail."

"He might'a been in jail, but he ain't no more."

"Doesn't matter now. Whoever he was, the son of a bitch is dead."

"I want to see his body," Felton said.

"How are you going to do that? He's at the bottom of the cliff, a hundred feet down," Deekus said.

"He killed Billy."

"Yeah, and now he's dead."

"He ain't dead till I see him dead," Felton said ominously.

Flailing at the side of the cliff with his hands as he went over, Quince had just managed to grab the roots of a small overhanging tree to arrest his fall. He hung there quietly for a minute, listening to the outlaws' discussion as they stood on the edge of the cliff above him, looking down into the void below. Not until he heard them leave did he start trying to find a way out of his predicament. Finding purchase for his hands and feet wherever he could—in crevices, scrub trees, and brush—he managed to work his way down until he reached the bottom, some one hundred feet below. The moon came out from behind the clouds for a moment, and Quince discerned a well-used animal trail. He started running, forcing himself onward for another quarter hour. Finally, assuming that he was safe, the exhausted young man crawled into the middle of a thick stand of bushes, where he collapsed, curled up, and went to sleep.

Chapter Three

Rachel Kincaid opened her eyes and looked through the window of the railroad car and smiled with pleasure. The dawn sky was streaked with various shades of red, gold, and purple, and she had almost forgotten how wonderful the sunrises could be in Wyoming. Toying with a lock of her long, dark hair, she lay in her berth listening to the rhythmic clack the wheels made on the tracks, enjoying the patterns and colors of the breathtakingly beautiful, ever-changing sky.

No! She suddenly reprimanded herself, her light blue eyes flashing and her fair skin flushing. *I won't enjoy this!*

Angrily turning her head away from the window, she stared at the heavy green curtain that covered her berth. She refused to allow herself to be seduced by the rugged beauty of this land, for she knew that this country had little to offer other than brutal winters, blistering summers, hard work, and heartbreak.

Two years ago her father had sent her away to a school in Boston. The school was at the forefront of women's education, and while there, she had come to regard herself in an entirely new light. Additionally, she got a glimpse of a world that she had not even known existed: She discovered great libraries that contained more books than she could read in a hundred lifetimes; she visited museums to view some of the world's greatest art treasures; she attended concerts where the music was so beautiful it could rival the heavenly hosts, and she dreamed that one day, perhaps even she would be a member of such an orchestra; she saw plays and ballets performed by the foremost artists of the day; and she attended lectures given by the most learned men in the world.

Boston had indoor plumbing and gas lights, steam heat and elevators, hospitals where medical miracles were being performed, and even telephones. After two years, Rachel had come to believe that Boston was the only place to be, and she wondered why anyone would ever want to live in a place like Wyoming.

Then she had received a letter from her father explaining that a very difficult winter had dealt the ranch such serious financial setbacks that he could no longer afford to keep her in the school. Stoically, Rachel looked upon that as but one more of the penalties Wyoming extracted from those people crazy or stubborn enough to choose to live there.

In the letter, Rachel's father asked her to please come back home, and Rachel reluctantly complied. But in her own mind she was going home only long enough to convince her father to sell his ranch and return East with her. In Boston, her mother and father could live quite comfortably for the rest of their lives on the money they could get from selling the ranch.

On the other side of the heavy green curtain that covered her berth and afforded her some privacy, Rachel heard the porter walking through the cars, announcing that breakfast was now being served in the dining car. With a deep sigh, she roused herself and struggled into her clothes; then she climbed down from the berth and hurried to the washroom at the end of the car.

"Ah, dear, there you are!"

Kate O'Leary, a smile lighting her strikingly lovely face, greeted Rachel as she arrived in the dining car a few minutes later. The sunlight streaming through the window dappled Kate's auburn hair, making it look like burnished copper. Kate's seven-year-old daughter, Lucy, was sitting beside her mother, and Rachel smiled at the young girl as she sat down.

"Well, don't you look pretty this morning, Lucy," Rachel said.

Lucy smiled shyly.

"Lucy, what do you say?"

"Thank you, Miss Kincaid," Lucy said self-consciously.

"You're welcome."

"Today is the day, Miss Kincaid," Lucy said. "We get home today."

"Not quite, Lucy," Kate reminded her daughter. "Remember, we still have a long stagecoach ride ahead of us."

"Yes, but at least we're in Wyoming," Lucy said. "I'm really glad to be back. I didn't like Philadelphia. I don't know why we moved there."

"I told you why we moved there, dear. I didn't think I could run the hotel by myself, and I needed some way to make a living for us. So I took a job acting as housekeeper for Mr. Dawson."

"I'm glad you don't have to work for Mr. Dawson anymore," Lucy said.

Kate smiled. "I'm glad, too, sweetheart."

Kate had told Rachel about her experience in Philadelphia, and how Mr. Dawson, a wealthy lawyer, expected Kate's services to include more than just keeping the house.

"I might have entertained the notion if he had

suggested marriage," Lucy confided, "but marriage was not in his plans."

Rachel and Kate had met as they changed trains in Omaha. Before she had left Wyoming, Rachel had known the O'Learys, for Kate and her husband had run a small hotel and restaurant in Antelope Springs, the closest town to the ranch where Rachel was raised.

It was Kate's husband who was killed by Deekus Tombs, when he attempted to stop the robbery in Theresa. Not wanting to run the hotel herself, Kate had rented out the lobby to the Wyoming Coach and Express Company to use as their depot. Then she packed up her clothes and some personal belongings and took Lucy with her to Philadelphia. She chose Philadelphia because it was the city of her birth. It wasn't exactly as if she was returning to the bosom of her family, though. She had only one cousin who still lived in Philadelphia, and they had never met.

Kate realized that she had made a mistake almost immediately. She missed having her own home, she missed Wyoming, and she missed her friends. So when her job didn't work out as she had planned, she bought train tickets for herself and her daughter back to Wyoming.

When Kate and Rachel met on the train in Omaha, two former acquaintances finding each other amidst a sea of strangers, they immediately renewed their friendship. They proved to be wonderful company for each other during the long train ride. The two women chatted cheerily through breakfast, until Rachel noticed that Lucy had eaten very little.

"Lucy, I don't believe it," Rachel teased. "You, the world's greatest pancake eater, are passing up your last morning's stack of them?"

"I guess I'm just not very hungry, Miss Kincaid," Lucy answered.

Kate put a solicitous hand on her daughter's forehead. "I don't know, Rachel, she was complaining of a stomachache during the night," Kate said. "It may have been something she ate."

"Yes, or perhaps it's motion sickness," Rachel suggested. "I've observed that it can sometimes occur even if you've been riding for several days with no previous ill effects."

"Yes," Kate agreed, nodding. "Perhaps so." She smiled. "If that's what it is, she'll certainly have the opportunity to recover soon enough. The conductor told me a short while ago that we'll be arriving in Rock Creek in about an hour, so we'll finally be done riding trains." She studied Rachel for a moment, then suggested, "You know, my dear, you might want to reconsider your dress. While it's most becoming, and I do so admire the beautiful lacework on the collar and cuffs, it seems a bit . . . well, a bit too civilized for a long stagecoach ride."

The young woman looked down at her dress and then at the sensible blue wool shirtwaist with buttons up the front that Kate was wearing. Rachel touched a napkin to her lips and smiled at her table companions. "Well, you are absolutely right. I don't know what I was thinking." Then she laughed ruefully and declared, "I guess after two years of getting used to city transportation, I had put out of my mind how rough-and-tumble stagecoaches are. I'd better get back to my berth and change. I'll see you soon." She looked at Lucy. "And I sure hope you are feeling much better when I see you again."

"I hope so, too," Lucy said.

In the Pair-O-Dice Saloon in Rock Creek, Wyoming, the gambler took his beer over to a table and sat down. A thin layer of tobacco smoke just beneath the ceiling drifted and curled through the room, then collected in a small cloud above the gambler's table. Noticing it, he wondered if it might be the portent of some doom; he shook his head to drive the thought away.

Damon Parker was in his early forties, handsome in a rather tired and jaded way. But unlike most of the other men in the saloon, Damon was clean—in fact, almost fastidiously so—and his dark and onyx eyes were mirrored by the fashionable, even elegant black clothes he always wore. There was also an air about him, a way he had of seemingly being detached from everything and everyone . . . even himself.

Damon was engaged in a little three-card monte game with a man named Zarachore, a rancher who was a good customer of the saloon. It was a simple game, not too unlike the game of finding the pea under the shell. In this case, however, Zarachore had to find the ace after watching Damon deftly shift the cards around in front of him.

Three times Zarachore tried his luck, and three times Damon won. Then, another saloon patron engaged Damon in conversation. This was by design, for Zarachore had arranged for this other patron to divert Damon's attention away from the three cards, just for a moment.

With Damon's back turned, Zarachore reached across the table and put a small, barely noticeable crease on one corner of the ace. Let Damon switch the cards around all he wanted now; Zarachore would make no attempt whatever to follow his swift hands. He would simply select the card with the creased corner.

"You going to play cards, or are you going to talk all day?" Zarachore asked.

Damon turned back to the table. "Why, I'm going to play cards, Mr. Zarachore," Damon said, smiling easily.

"Only this time, let's bet some real money," Zarachore suggested. He put ten twenty-dollar gold pieces on the table.

"That's a pretty steep bet for a little friendly game like this, isn't it?" Damon asked.

"If it's too rich for you, just say so," Zarachore said.

Damon drummed his fingers on the card table for a moment. The size of Zarachore's bet had caught the attention of some of the other patrons of the saloon and what had started as a quiet game between the two men suddenly turned into a spectator sport as others now crowded around to watch.

"So, what are you going to do, gamblin' man?" someone in the crowd asked. "Fish, or cut bait?"

Damon had been in Rock Creek for two weeks now and he had been so successful at the poker tables that it was getting increasingly difficult to find someone to play with. Even this game, which required nothing more than a pair of attentive eyes to watch him as he shuffled the cards around, had few takers until Zarachore approached him a short time earlier.

"Well, if you don't want to play . . ." Zarachore said, reaching to the middle of the table to pull his stack of coins back.

"No, no, I'll play," Damon said, reaching into his own pocket to bring out enough money to match the bet. As he put his own money on the table alongside the stack of gold coins, Zarachore took one last look at the creased card. So far, Damon hadn't noticed it, and how could he? It was so subtle a crease that it was barely discernable, even to Zarachore, and he was the one who put it there.

Damon picked up the three cards and began shuffling them around. Zarachore looked over at his partner in this setup and nodded. Damon put the cards down on the table, then began moving them around, in and out, over and under, with such lightning speed that the cards were nearly a blur. Then he stopped and the three cards lay in front of him, waiting for Zarachore to pick the ace.

With a smug smile, Zarachore reached across the table to make his selection . . . then suddenly he froze and the smile left his face. His hand hung suspended over the table.

"Go on, Zarachore, pick out the ace. You can do it," one of the men in the crowd said.

Zarachore stared at the three cards with a sickly expression on his face. All three cards now bore that same creased corner. Damon had not only seen it, he had somehow managed to duplicate it on the other cards with such exactness, that Zarachore had no idea which card he had marked.

"It's hard, isn't it?" Damon asked with a sly grin. "When they all look alike, I mean."

"I know what you mean," Zarachore seethed. In desperation, Zarachore turned up one of the cards. It was a jack.

"Damn!" Zarachore said.

"Sorry," Damon said easily, reaching for the money in the center of the table.

"Wait a minute!" Zarachore said. "I don't believe the ace is even on the table."

"Sure it is. I'll show you," Damon said. He started to reach for one of the cards.

"Wait a minute, I'll turn it over," Zarachore said. "For all I know you have an ace palmed. You can make it appear anywhere you want."

"All right, you turn it over."

Zarachore reached for the card Damon had started for and flipped it over. It was the ace.

"Damn," Zarachore said.

"Oh, and, Mr. Zarachore, as far as my being able to make an ace appear anywhere, check the band of your hat."

"What?" Zarachore asked.

"Your hat," Damon said. "Check in the hatband."

Zarachore took off his hat and examined it.

There, sticking out of the hat band, was an ace of clubs.

"Well, I'll be damned!" Zarachore sputtered. "How did that get there?"

The others in the saloon laughed uproariously as Damon picked up the money.

Chapter Four

Deekus Tombs was standing on the side of the cliff where they had seen the man go over last night. Idly, he tossed a rock from hand to hand while the others came back from their search. Seeing them return, the outlaw dropped the rock. "Find anything?" he asked.

"Nary a trace," Hawk Peters answered. "I don't know who he was, but he got away cleaner'n a whistle."

"How the hell could he have survived that fall?" Deekus asked.

"Looks like he grabbed aholt of a tree, then clumb down that way," Hawk said.

Deekus looked over the group. "Where's Felton?"

"He took out after 'im. He said nobody was going to kill his brother and get away with it."

"Were there tracks to follow?"

Hawk shook his head. "That's pure rock

down there, Deekus. You could as soon track a bird through the air.''

"What are we going to do about Felton?" Silver asked.

"We ain't goin' to do nothin' about him," Deekus said.

"You think we can pull this off without the Pogue boys?" Hawk asked.

"And what about his share of the money?" Silver added.

Deekus snorted. "How hard is it to hold up a stage?" he asked. "Won't be nobody on it but women and drummers. Besides, without the Pogues, ever'body's share just got bigger."

"Yeah!" Prescott said. "Yeah, who needs 'em, anyway?"

"Come on, boys, let's get a move on. We got some ridin' to do to be in position to pull this job."

Quince shielded his eyes and watched the bird. It was the fourth one he had seen alight at a particular spot. If all the birds had been of the same kind, he would have presumed that there was a nest there, three-quarters of the way up the side of the rocky cliff. But they had all been different species, and that could only mean one thing: The birds were going to water!

Putting his hands on his hips, Quince studied the sheer rock wall. The place that was drawing the birds was at least two hundred feet above the ground. Though it would be a hard climb, he believed he could do it.

It would be easy, he thought, if he just had a rope. Then he mocked himself, saying aloud, "Yeah, and if wishes were wings, frogs wouldn't bump their asses when they jump." He took a deep breath and then let out a long sigh and started up the side of the cliff.

It was very hard going. When Quince had been at it for roughly half an hour, he looked up toward his destination and groaned. It did not seem as if he had gained an inch. However, when he looked back down toward the ground, he realized that he was making some progress, for by now he was dangerously high.

Clinging to the side of the cliff, he moved only when he had a secure handhold or foothold, precarious though they might be. Sweat poured into his eyes, and the thirst that had driven him to this state of desperation had been greatly intensified by his efforts. If he was wrong—if the birds were not leading him to water—he had made his situation even worse. He was so desperate for water now that he could feel his tongue swelling in his mouth.

Abruptly, Quince came to what appeared to be an impasse. He had progressed four-fifths of the way around a very large outcropping, but now he was stopped because he was unable to find another foothold. Clinging with hands that were fast becoming painfully swollen, he tried to figure out what to do next.

After five minutes, he reluctantly decided to start back down to see if he could find another way around the obstacle. Reaching for the handhold he had surrendered a few minutes earlier, he then put his foot down on the small, slate outcropping that had supported his weight on the way up. This time, however, the slate failed, and with a sickening sensation in his stomach, Quince felt himself falling. He threw himself against the side, and the jagged rocks scraped and tore at his flesh as he slid downward.

He flailed against the wall with his hands, and after a drop of some fifteen feet, his bloodied hands found the trunk of a juniper bush growing out of the cliff. Grabbing the tree, which, thankfully, supported his weight, Quince once again found himself hanging in midair. His heart was pounding furiously as he looked down between his feet and the rocky ground some hundred and fifty feet below. The piece of the slate outcropping that had broken under his weight was still falling. Seconds later he saw a puff of dust as it smashed against the ground, and a second later he heard the sound as it broke apart upon impact.

Suddenly his body shifted downward, and he felt the tree giving way. Cold sweat broke out on his brow and his palms. Frantic, Quince examined the cliff face and saw that about four feet away to his right was a narrow shelf. If he could just gain that shelf, he would be all right. He took a deep breath and then swung his feet to the right and up . . . and missed. He felt his body slip another inch as the juniper's roots pulled out a bit more.

Dear God, he prayed, *don't let me die like this! Not without clearing my and my brother's names!*

Straining with all his might, he swung his leg up again, but again he narrowly missed. He tried several more times, and each time the increased weight on the juniper bush pulled the roots farther out. Quince rested momentarily, listening to his pulse pounding in his ears. Then he tried again, and this time he caught the ledge with the heel of his boot. Breathing another silent prayer, he then slowly worked himself up and away from the juniper tree, until his knees were also on the ledge. Finally, he let go of the tree and pushed up slowly against the rock face until at last he was safely on the ledge.

He sat there unmoving for a few minutes, gasping for air and letting his heartbeat slow to normal. When he had caught his wind and was ready to move on, he looked around and got a pleasant surprise. Rising up from the ledge was a "chimney," a narrow chute that shot straight up the side of the cliff. This natural shaft was studded with rocks in such a way as to almost form a ladder, and within a minute after starting up, Quince recovered the distance he had lost in the fall. The nauseating fear that had overtaken him earlier was now gone, and he climbed easily, finding footholds and handholds so conveniently located that it was almost as if they had been placed there for just such a purpose.

Finally Quince reached the spot where he had seen the birds alight, and he managed to leave the chimney and climb over to a large, flat rock. Just above the rock was a shallow cave, and there, trapped in a cool, shaded reservoir at the bottom of that cave, was a pool of water. With a happy shout, Quince dunked his head under and drank deeply.

Back in Rock Springs, Damon Parker sat at the same table where half an hour earlier, he had won two hundred dollars in gold from Coley Zarachore. The game had been unusual in that Zarachore was the one who had approached him, and had, in fact, suggested the game. Damon much preferred poker, but he could find fewer and fewer players now who would match their skills against his.

Presently, with no one to play with, he was entertaining himself by spreading the cards out, then adroitly turning over the entire deck merely by passing a card back across the top.

After that he let the pasteboards cascade from hand to hand, his long fingers working so adeptly that it almost appeared as if magic were at work. Then he shuffled them and began dealing an imaginary poker game. After each deal, he would turn over all the hands, noting the fall of certain cards. Then he would pick them up, reshuffle, and deal again.

A train whistle sounded outside, breaking the silence of the room, and the bartender pulled out his pocket watch and looked at it rather pointedly, almost as if he were responsible for the arrivals and departures of the Union Pacific trains. At the same time, a couple of men at the bar nodded at each other, passing a silent signal between them. Suddenly Damon Parker heard the double click of a revolver being cocked, and he felt the cold metal of a gun barrel pressed against the back of his head.

"Mr. Gamblin' Man," a deep voice growled from behind him, "you're just too damned good with them there cards for the likes of Rock Creek."

Damon tensed and laid the cards down. He kept his hands palms-down on the table and in full view, a clear indication that he was not going to try anything. Clearing his throat, he asked, "Is skill against the law in this town?"

"Your kind of skill is," the unseen man behind him replied. "Now, we ain't exactly callin' you a cheater, you understand, 'cause if that's what you've been doin', there ain't none of us been able to catch you at it. Rest assured that if we had, we'd be stringin' you up about now, instead of doin' what we're doin'."

"I see," Damon said, able to breathe a bit easier. If they were not going to lynch him, then it seemed less likely that they were going to shoot him. Calmly, he began picking his cards up from the table. "I take it, then, that I am being run out of town?"

"That you are, mister," the man replied. "I reckon you just heard the train whistle?"

"I did."

"That train'll be standin' at the depot for half an hour, then it heads on west. There will be a stage leavin' the depot goin' north at about the same time. We don't much care which form of transportation it is you choose, but you are damn sure goin' to be on one of 'em."

Damon grinned laconically and straightened his string tie. "Well, since I've about exhausted my welcome along the entire Union Pacific route, I'm going to have to start looking for virgin territory. Therefore, I guess I'll take the stagecoach north. May I at least go over to the hotel to get my bag?"

"No need for that, Gamblin' Man. We got it for you." So saying, the man dropped a leather valise beside Damon's chair.

"May I turn around, please? I would like to see the composition of this farewell committee."

"Sure, go ahead, turn around," the man agreed. "Ain't none of us got any reason to hide from the likes of you."

When Damon turned, he saw that there were at least six men with the spokesman. He recognized every one of them . . . and had, in fact, played cards with each of them.

"Ah, George," he said to the man holding the gun. "Is it because you couldn't fill an inside straight that you decided to take your frustrations out in this way? And you, Phil?" He shook his head slowly, berating the man. "Breaking a pair of kings to go for a flush when the pair alone would have won the hand. Oh, and we mustn't forget Charley, a man who thinks bluster and bluff will compensate for an inadequate knowledge of poker."

"That's enough of all that," a well-dressed man said. Damon recognized him as Marcus Pendarrow, a businessman who had played often, and lost often. "You're trying to get us to fight among ourselves," Pendarrow snapped. "But your tricks won't work. We are men of resolve, and we intend to see that you leave town."

Damon dropped his cards into his jacket pocket and leaned down to pick up his bag.

"Well, then, you gentlemen of . . . resolve . . .

I bid you good day," he said, nodding graciously at his send-off committee. Standing, he strode quickly across the room, pushed through the batwing doors, and stepped out into the afternoon sun. He stood there for a moment, blinking at the unaccustomed brightness, and then headed for the depot a block away. This was a routine procedure with him by now. Rock Creek was not the first town he had ever been asked to leave.

As the train rattled to a stop at the Rock Creek station, Rachel Kincaid and Kate O'Leary gazed out the window, each lost in her own thoughts. Both women looked out at the same scene: a station platform stacked with crates and boxes and, beyond that, a dirt street and a scattering of perhaps thirty low, unpainted, clapboard buildings. But though both saw the same things, they perceived them differently.

To Rachel, this was the exact opposite of the life she had been living and enjoying in Boston, and she wondered if it was possible now for her to return to such a place. Kate, on the other hand, welcomed the sun-bleached buildings, the dust-covered men and women, and the heat waves radiating off the endless, empty plains. They were old and familiar things to her, and they had tightened their hold so securely around her heart that, seeing them now, she knew she would never leave them again.

The depot was a flurry of activity and noise. On the platform, men yelled at each other as a steel-wheeled car was rolled up to the baggage car to load and unload suitcases, crates, and mailbags. Here the train also took on water, precipitating a great deal of banging and clanging of tank covers and waterspouts as the water tank was filled. The fireman kept the fire stoked and the steam going, and the rhythmic opening and closing of the valves as the pressure repeatedly built up and then vented away sounded remarkably like the laborious breathing of some great beast of burden.

In addition to those people manning the depot and the passengers arriving and departing—plus those meeting them or sending them off—dozens of townspeople, to whom the arrival of the train was a major event, crowded the depot. This particular train also corresponded with the arrival and departure of the stagecoach heading north, lending an even more festive air to the occasion.

A few of the more urbane transcontinental passengers, those going on through to San Francisco, got off the train to stretch their legs and have a look around. Standing on the platform, they gawked at the local men lounging against the wall of the depot, their hips adorned with cartridge belts and pistols. The visitors stared unabashedly at the locals, for these were real "cowboys" of the type they had only read about, and they watched closely, waiting for the sudden explosion of temper that might lead to one of the famous gunfights that they presumed occurred regularly in towns like this one.

A few moments later, when a drayman popped his whip with the explosiveness of a pistolshot, several of the Easterners jumped. Their eyes wide in fright and fascination, they drew closer together, the better to stay out of the path of any flying projectiles from the fracas they were sure had broken out.

Laughing softly, Kate remarked to Rachel, "I suppose none of these city slickers have ever heard a bullwhip before."

"I suppose not," Rachel agreed, also laughing. Though she had lived with Easterners for the past two years and had even come to regard herself as one of them, she couldn't help but smirk at their tenderfoot reaction, and she felt a sense of superiority over them. "I think, to such people, it is as if there is nothing between the cities of the East and San Francisco. The entire West from the Mississippi to the Pacific Ocean is nothing but pass-through country. It's almost as if we don't even exist."

"Mama, I don't feel very good," Lucy suddenly moaned, holding her stomach.

"Oh, dear! I just don't know what's wrong with you," Kate replied, kneeling and putting a hand on her daughter's cheek. "Why don't you go over there and lie down on that bench while I get our stage tickets?"

"I'll stay with her until you get the tickets, then I'll get mine," Rachel volunteered.

"Thank you. That's very sweet of you." Kate sighed, standing and drawing her cream-colored shawl tightly around her shoulders.

The ticket office for the stage line was inside the railroad depot. Kate arrived at the door leading into the building at the same time as a man dressed all in black. The man smiled graciously, stepped back, and opened the door for her.

"After you, madam," he said.

"Thank you."

Kate bought tickets for herself and Lucy to Antelope Springs, then with her head down, she stepped aside to put them in her reticule. As she pulled the drawstring tight, about to head out of the depot, she was surprised to hear the man who had been behind her buy a ticket to the same destination. Turning, she saw that it was the same man in black who had held open the door.

She smiled at him, asking, "Do you live in

Antelope Springs?" Then she laughed nervously. "I'm sorry. I know it was rude of me to inquire, but I used to live in Antelope Springs and now I'm going back home. I was just wondering if you had moved in during my absence."

"Madam, if you live there, then I can't think of anyone I would rather be neighbors with," the man said, touching the brim of his flat-crowned black hat as he smiled at her. "But the truth is, I'll be visiting your fair town for the first time."

"Oh," Kate murmured. She found the man intriguingly handsome, and the more she talked with him, the more certain she was that she was making a fool of herself. "Well, I, uh, I'm sure you will enjoy it," she said. "If you'll excuse me now, I must see to my daughter. You see, I'm a widow and—" Kate stopped in midsentence and felt her face burning in embarrassment. She wished a giant pit would open up beneath her feet and swallow her whole. Why had she told him she was a widow? How obvious could a person be?

But the man smiled with seemingly genuine pleasure and said, "My name is Damon Parker. May I inquire as to your name?"

"Kate. That is, Kate O'Leary."

"Mrs. O'Leary, as we'll be traveling companions, and as you are without a husband, I do hope you will call on me if you should need any assistance."

"Uh, yes, thank you," Kate mumbled, unable to meet his gaze. "But I'm sure I will have no difficulty."

"Nevertheless, madam, I shall remain at your service."

Kate nodded and then scurried to the door.

Waiting for Kate to return, Rachel saw a tall, slim young man walk out of the depot building. For a moment she thought she recognized him, and she half stood and raised her hand to call out to him. Then the young man turned his head, enabling Rachel to see him more clearly, and she realized he was not who she thought he was. But then, of course, how could he have been? The person she had thought he might be was in prison.

Rachel didn't want to believe it when her father wrote to her of Quince Fremont's troubles. But he also sent newspaper clippings of the incident, so she knew it must be true. Rachel and Quince had danced together once at a rancher's social, and he seemed polite and very attentive. That evening, as young women sometimes do, she wrote his name several times on a sheet of paper, including, "Mrs. Quince Fremont." Then, boldly, she wrote, "Rachel Fremont. Jason Fremont. Sally Fremont." Jason and Sally were the children they would have together in the future, of course.

But Quince never called on her again after the social. Then once, when she was in Antelope Springs, she saw him entering a saloon with a painted woman hanging onto his arm. When she got back home that evening she found the piece of paper she had so foolishly covered with her imaginative scribbling. Wadding it up into a small ball, she tossed it into the pot-bellied iron stove.

Not wanting to think anymore about it, she glanced away from the handsome young cowboy and began talking with Lucy O'Leary about the impending stagecoach ride.

Chapter Five

Inside one of the houses on the other side of town, in the small residential section of Rock Creek, Ethan Matthews stood at the side of his bed, hurriedly packing his suitcase under the watchful eye of his wife, Cindy. Taking a shirt from a drawer, Matthews unfolded it, then refolded it, making absolutely certain that every crease was in the right place and that no new wrinkles were being formed.

A short, thin man in his early forties, Matthews had blue eyes, brown hair, and a small, closely cropped mustache. He was extremely fastidious, a quality even more evidenced by the great care he was taking with his packing.

Suddenly the bedsprings groaned in protest as his wife shifted.

"Ethan," she said.

"Yes."

"Ethan, look at me."

Obeying, Matthews found that his wife had

removed her dress and her undergarments as well. They were hanging from the big brass ball on one side of the headboard. Cindy was a very large, relatively plain-looking woman, and while some men might be partial to her generous shape, with its abundant breasts, Matthews was not one of those men.

Matthews sighed and closed his eyes. "Cindy, for God's sake, cover yourself," he muttered in a low, flat voice. "You shouldn't be seen like that. You are positively indecent."

"Naked is the way we came into this world, Ethan. There is absolutely nothing indecent about it," Cindy protested.

"Men and women do not come into this world with fully matured bodies," Matthews countered.

Cindy's countenance grew cold. "Perhaps not, but I am your wife, and there is nothing indecent about a man seeing his own wife naked."

"The only time a man should ever see his wife naked is at night, when he can't see her at all," Matthews said.

"Don't you love me?" she pleaded.

"Of course I do," he answered without expression or conviction. Looking away from her, he went back to packing his suitcase.

Matthews was aware of Cindy's eyes on him, watching his every movement. Sneaking a glance at her, he found her looking at him with hurt eyes, and after a moment, she opened her mouth to speak.

Hesitantly, she said, "This pains me, but I have to ask it. Ethan, would you love me if my father wasn't the president of the bank and you weren't his chief clerk?"

"Cindy, what kind of a question is that?" Matthews demanded, sidestepping an answer. "Why, you degrade yourself, your father, and me, by asking that kind of question."

"I'm sorry, but I can't help it," Cindy replied. Her eyes misted over with tears. "Ethan, I realize I am not a very pretty woman. But I am a loving woman, and I could be a good wife to you if only you would let me." Shamelessly, she ran her hand down the side of her body, letting it slide over the curve of her hip. "I can be very good to you," she added in a sultry tone.

"You are good to me, Cindy, and I have no complaints about our relationship," Matthews responded, his voice flat and cool. Putting his last pair of trousers into the suitcase, he closed it and buckled it shut.

"When will you be back?" Cindy asked.

"One never knows about these things," Matthews said as he put on his brown pin-striped jacket, then tugged at the cuffs of his shirt. "Perhaps as long as a month, perhaps longer. Your father has charged me with a very serious responsibility. As you know, this past winter was extremely hard in northern Wyoming, and many of the cattlemen were badly hurt. I will be handling a series of emergency loans, which is why I will be carrying a large quantity of money with me, one of the largest shipments ever transferred by the Rock Creek Bank."

"Yes, I understand," Cindy murmured. Suddenly she smiled and sat up on the bed. "Ethan?"

"Yes, what is it?"

"What if I come to Antelope Springs with you?"

Matthews's face blanched. "Come with me? Are you crazy?"

"No, I'm not crazy," Cindy replied, unable to keep the hurt from her voice. "What is to keep me here? If you're going to be up there for an entire month, we could find a place to live, a small house perhaps, and you wouldn't have to stay in a hotel."

"No, it's out of the question."

"But won't you just—"

"I said it is out of the question," the little bank clerk repeated, holding his hand up to prevent her from arguing any further.

"I just thought it would be nice," Cindy suggested.

Matthews forced himself to smile at her. "Yes, but think how much nicer it will be when I come home after being gone for so long," he said. "I have to have something to look forward to that will bring me back. Otherwise, I might decide I want to stay up there."

Cindy's eyes opened wide in surprise. Then she smiled when he laughed, indicating that he was merely joking.

Brushing away her tears, she asked in a small voice, "Really, Ethan? Will you really be looking forward to coming back home to me?"

"Yes, of course I will be." Matthews took his watch from his pocket, opened it and examined the face, then snapped it shut. "I must be going now. The stagecoach will be leaving soon."

"Kiss me good-bye."

Walking up to the head of the bed, Matthews leaned over to give his wife a light peck on the cheek. Abruptly, she grabbed his hand and placed it against her naked breast, holding it fast.

"Good-bye, Cindy," Matthews muttered, pulling his hand away as if it had touched something unclean, then walking quickly from the room. When he was safely out in the hallway, he wiped his hand on the leg of his trousers, a look of distaste on his thin mouth. He sighed and then hurried down the stairs and took his overcoat from the peg on the mirrored coat stand at the bottom of the stairs. He put on the coat, checked his appearance in the mirror, and left the house, walking briskly toward the depot, where the money from the bank would be waiting for him.

Across town, in Sheriff Gerald Farrell's office, Will Jordan picked up the old blue coffeepot from the stove and poured himself a cup of coffee. Like the man he was visiting, Will also wore a sheriff's badge. He was the sheriff of Crook County, far to the north, working out of the small town of Antelope Springs. He had brought three prisoners to Rock Creek a few days earlier, and they were now languishing in the back of the Carbon County-Rock Creek jail.

Having been a lawman for more than half of his almost fifty-eight years, the tall, solidly built Jordan fit into his profession like a pair of old boots. He had an easy way about him and was usually as unruffled as his slicked-down gray hair, although his clear blue eyes could bore right through a man, especially a man on the wrong side of the law.

"Well, now, here is something interesting," Farrell said, as he went through the messages on his desk.

"What's that?" Jordan asked, taking a drink of his coffee.

"Quince Fremont has escaped prison."

"The hell you say."

"That's what it says here."

"When?"

"Just a few days ago. They haven't even had time to put out reward posters on him, but the governor has already authorized a reward of twenty-five hundred dollars."

"That's a lot of money," Jordan said. "With that kind of money, a fella could damn near retire."

Farrell put the messages down, then walked over to pour himself a cup of coffee. "You know him, don't you Will? As I recollect, you testified for him at his trial."

"Wasn't much of a testimony," Jordan said. "All I could say was that I knew Quince and his brother, and that they had been good citizens with no run-ins with the law. I thought it seemed a little out of character for them to be robbing a bank . . . especially with the likes of Deekus Tombs." He chuckled. "I said if those two boys ever decided to go into bank robbing, they would have gone into it by themselves."

"I'll bet that went over well with the judge," Farrell said with a little laugh.

"Did he hurt anyone?"

"What?"

"Fremont. When he escaped, did he hurt or kill anyone?"

"No. Somehow he managed to get his cell door open, then he escaped through a window. He left a dummy on his bed in his cell, so they didn't even discover it until the next day."

"How'd he get out of the prison?"

"Nobody knows for sure, but they think he may have somehow hidden himself in a wagon that left late that night."

"Sounds like a pretty resourceful man," Will Jordan said. He put his cup down. "He's prob'ly halfway to California, by now. Or at least, I hope so."

"You hope so?"

"Like I said, he's a good man, and I don't think he pulled that robbery with Tombs. If Fremont's smart, he'll go to California and lose himself there."

"Do you think he will? Go to California, I mean."

Jordan sighed and shook his head. "In the trial, he insisted that Deekus Tombs and his men jumped him and his brother. They killed his brother, knocked him out, then put the shirts from two of the gang on them to frame them. If that's true, he won't be going to California. I reckon he'll be looking for Deekus Tombs."

"Deekus's been working up in your territory again, hasn't he?"

"Yes."

"Then if you are right about Quince Fremont, he'll be up there, too."

Jordan nodded. "I'd hate being the one to have to take him in."

"Would you take him in? I mean, feeling the way you do about him?"

Jordan looked down at the badge on his shirt. "I've worn this piece of tin a long time. I can't turn my back on it now. If I run across Fremont, I'll take him in."

"And collect the reward?"

"I have to admit, it would feel a little like blood money, but I would be honor-bound to take him in, and if I did that, it would be foolish not to collect the reward," Will said. "Twenty-five hundred dollars is a lot of money to a man who makes forty a month."

"How would you like to make an extra seventy-five dollars?" Farrell asked.

"Seventy-five dollars? Doing what?"

"Doing just what you are going to do anyway. Ride the stage to Antelope Springs."

Jordan squinted his eyes. "I don't get it," he said. "What are you proposing?"

Farrell laughed. "Nothing dishonest, so you can put your mind at ease on that score," he said. "Will Jordan, you have been a lawman too long. You are a very suspicious soul."

"It has served me well over the years," Jordan replied. "Now . . . what about this seventy-five dollars?"

Farrell walked over to the front door of his office, opened it, then looked both ways up and down the street. Satisfied that no one was lurking about, he closed the door then returned to his desk. Jordan watched the whole thing with an air of curiosity.

"Nobody knows it yet, but there is going to be a large shipment of money on that stage. A very large shipment. The bank here is sending one hundred thousand dollars up to the bank at Antelope Springs."

Jordan let out a low whistle. "One hundred thousand dollars? My God, I can't even imagine that much money. That is an absolute fortune."

"Yes, it is. And the bank has offered a bonus of one hundred dollars to any deputy I can get who will ride up with the shipment. Now, the thing is, a deputy would have to go up there and come back . . . but since you are going anyway, it seems to me like you would be ideal for the job. If you was to agree to act as my deputy, I could pay you three-quarters of this bonus, or seventy-five dollars, and pocket the rest for myself. I mean, you're going to be on the stage anyway, so, what do you say?"

Will Jordan took another sip of coffee and studied his fellow lawman over the rim of his cup. Farrell was correct: He *was* going to be on that stage, whether he accepted the deal or not, so if he could pick up a little extra for it, why not? And since he was going anyway, he could afford to take less than a special deputy, thus, leaving some money left over for Sheriff Farrell, while leaving Farrell with all of his deputies.

"All right," Jordan finally said. He laughed and stuck out his hand. "It seems too good an offer to refuse. You've got yourself a deal."

Chapter Six

The engineer blew two long whistles, the signal that he was releasing the brakes, and the train began rolling forward, steam gushing out of the drive cylinders on each side of the engine. Dozens of good-byes were exchanged between those people who remained behind on the station platform and those who were on board, shouting to each other through the open windows.

"Well, there it goes," Kate said, relief in her voice. She sighed. "It seemed like we were on that thing forever." Then she laughed and gestured across the platform, adding, "Though I guess by tomorrow morning, I'll wish we were back on it instead of the stage."

A Concord stagecoach was parked near the station. Tough and sturdy from its seasoned white ash spokes to its oxide boot, it had no springs but was suspended on layers of leather straps, called throughbraces, making for a rough ride. The body of the coach was green, and the lettering on the doors was yellow, although the paint was tired and the colors faded—the coach was at least ten years old and had seen a great deal of use during its lifetime. Still, it was well maintained, as evidenced by the neat and very skillful patchwork done to a few places on the coach body and the leather seats inside. The coach belonged to the Wyoming Coach and Express Company, a stage line that connected outlying settlements throughout Wyoming with the railroads that passed through the territory.

Six fresh horses were led around to the stage, the hostlers speaking quietly and reassuringly to the animals as they began readying them for the trip ahead. As Rachel watched the men working with the team, she recalled a day in May, two years earlier. That was the day she left home.

She remembered that she had gone out to watch the sun rise one more time over her father's ranch, and even now she could remember how it looked as it climbed higher into the clear, blue sky above the mountains. Looking down upon the sweeping grandeur of the valley, its timbered foothills covered with blue pine and splashed with the rainbow colors of wild spring blooms, Rachel had thought then that her father's ranch was the most beautiful place in the world. She had been sure that neither Boston,

nor anyplace else in the East—or for that matter
in all the world—could possibly offer anything
to compete with this.

She got up before dawn, dressed in denim
trousers and a plaid shirt, then rode along the
familiar ridgeline, picking her way along a trail
that led to an overhanging precipice she had discovered as a little girl. It had become her "secret" place, a place where she came when she
wanted to be alone. From the height of the rocky
precipice, she could see the entire fifteen thousand acres of the finest rangeland in Wyoming
Territory. This was the Rocking K Ranch, which
included the main house where she lived with
her mother and father, the bunkhouses where
the forty ranch hands slept, and assorted other
buildings such as the barns, cookhouse, equip-
ment shed, and the smokehouse.

But the young brunette had gone up there to
think, not to enjoy the beautiful view. Her father
had made the arrangements for her to attend
school in the East.

"It will be good for you to see some of the
rest of the world," he told her. "You should
know that there are more places to be enjoyed
than Antelope Springs, Ten Sleep, and Rock
Creek."

As she had sat there that morning, she knew
she was closing the pages on one chapter of her

life, preparing to boldly go forward to what was yet to come.

In the valley below, a wispy pall of wood-smoke had spread its diaphanous haze over the cookhouse, and Rachel watched the cowboys saunter to the cookhouse for their morning meal. She had seen her father walk out to the barn and begin hitching up the rig that was to take her into town that morning to catch the stagecoach to Rock Creek, from where she would be able to connect with the train bound for the East.

She had known, even that morning, that she would be changed by her time in Boston, but she had no idea how much. As she looked down on her father's ranch, and the only home she had ever known, she could not imagine that there would ever come a time when she would want to say good-bye to this place forever. Yet that was exactly her thought as she sat here on the small wooden bench in the Rock Creek, Wyoming depot, waiting to board the stage that would take her back. For one odd moment, she almost wished that she felt differently, but then she recalled the excitement and vitality of life in Boston, and she knew that she would be going back as soon as she could.

By now the team was all hitched up, and the horses stood quietly in their harness, awaiting the orders that would set them to their labors, drawing the coach north over the plains and mountains of Wyoming. A baggage cart laden with the passengers' luggage was pushed from the train over to the stage. Employees of the depot then began loading the bags onto the coach. They were able to put most of the pieces in the boot, though two large trunks, one belonging to Kate and one belonging to Rachel, had to be lashed to the top.

"Well, it looks as if they have the stagecoach all loaded and ready for us," Kate O'Leary said when they were finished. "All we need now is a driver and we'll be on our way."

"Yes, I guess that's so," Rachel agreed.

Rachel experienced a wave of very ambivalent feelings. She wanted to see her mother and father again, but she felt that she no longer belonged here, as if she were trapped in a netherworld between Boston and her father's ranch. She looked over at the coach and saw that the two young men who had been loading the luggage were now walking away.

"I wonder where the driver is?" Kate asked.

Across the street from the depot, driver Gib Crabtree and his shotgun messenger, Beans Evans, were eating dinner at the City Pig Restaurant. Gib was a regular there, and he told everyone who would listen that he considered the City Pig the best eating establishment of any along his route.

Gib was fifty, with graying collar-length hair and a very long bushy mustache. He had been driving a stagecoach for over twenty years. Before that he had driven freight wagons, beginning his lifelong profession at the age of fifteen. Thirty-five years of sun and wind and heat and cold had weathered his face so that he looked much older than he was. But looking older did not mean he looked frail or infirm, for Gib Crabtree was a powerfully built man with wide shoulders and sinewy hands. His arms were strong enough to rein a six-horse team with authority, yet skilled enough to impart subtle instructions to each horse through its own "ribbon" when that was needed. He was without a doubt, most agreed, the best driver on the Wyoming Coach and Express Company's payroll.

Sitting at the table with Gib, Beans Evans was a man whose age was even more difficult to ascertain. He could have been anywhere from thirty-five to fifty, the determination not made easier by his sparse brown hair. A very short man, just a touch over five feet, Beans was whipcord tough. Evidence of that toughness was the long scar that started under his right eye, running down over his cheek in an ugly, blue puff of skin and ending in a fishhook just under the corner of his mouth. Many people had asked Beans how he got that scar, but he told a different story every time, so no one knew the truth of it.

"Gib, would you be wantin' some more 'taters?" Jane Pratt and her husband, Bill, ran the City Pig Restaurant, and the big-boned woman asked the question with a large, easy smile.

"Don't mind if I do," Gib answered, sliding his plate over to her as she raked a new batch of fried potatoes from a black, cast-iron skillet. "Nobody fries 'em as well as you, Jane."

Jane laughed. "Don't be tellin' Madge that," she quipped. "I wouldn't want your wife thinkin' you don't like her cookin'."

"Oh, Madge knows I like her cookin' all right," Gib said. "Fact is, the way I enjoy eatin', why, I reckon I would be kinda hard pressed to find somebody's cooking I don't like."

"What about you, Mr. Evans? You want anything else?" Jane asked the shotgun guard.

"Maybe a few more beans," he answered, not meeting her gaze. He picked up a porkchop bone and began gnawing.

"You know, Beans," Gib pointed out, "we're goin' to have to take the run all the way to Antelope Springs by ourselves. We was supposed to change at Theresa, but McCoy's wife is gettin' ready to foal, and he ain't goin' to leave her."

"That's all right. It don't bother me none," Beans said, shrugging. "You want to know the truth, I'd as soon go on up to Antelope Springs anyway, as spend time in Theresa. Ain't a damn thing a fella can do while he's awaitin' at Theresa for the next trip but sleep and swat flies."

"And smell the stink of oil," Gib said. "They got so much of that stuff oozing out of the ground that the water's bad."

Beans nodded in agreement. "Yeah, that stuff ain't good for nothin' but gettin' on you and killin' off the horses and cows that drink the polluted water."

"I can't help but feel sorry for all them poor beggars who homesteaded around there," Gib said. "They thought they was getting good farm- and ranch land, but wound up with all their water holes polluted with that stuff. What good is that land to 'em now?"

Jane came back from the kitchen carrying a pot of beans, and she spooned some onto Beans's plate. "You boys be careful during this trip," she instructed. "You're gonna have a lot of money ridin' with you."

"A lot of money? What do you mean?" Gib asked, perplexed.

Jane pointed her ladle through the front window to the outside. "You see that little feller there? The squinty-eyed hollow-chested little man who's walking toward the stagecoach?"

Gib focused on the man then laughed out loud at the accuracy of Jane's description. "Yes, I see him."

"That's Ethan Matthews," Jane explained. "He's head clerk over to the bank. He's married to Cindy Dempster, which means he's working for his father-in-law." She then proceeded to explain about the loans to the northern ranchers, concluding, "Matthews is taking the money up there personally, nearly a hundred thousand dollars, from what I hear." She suddenly looked around, making sure no one was listening, and then concluded in a conspiratorial voice, "Only, that's all supposed to be a secret."

"If it's a secret, how did you find out?" Gib asked.

Jane bent over the table and said quietly, "Well, Mr. Dempster and that Matthews fella have their lunch in here near 'bout ever' day, and I overhear them talking from time to time. That's how come I know about it."

"Well, I'm glad to hear of it," Gib said. "There was lots of fine folks hurt by that bad winter, and I know they'll be glad to see that some money's comin' in to tide 'em over."

"That may be, but if you ask me, the bank here sure picked out a weasel to handle all the dealings for them," Jane muttered. " 'Course, as I say, Ethan Matthews is Mr. Dempster's son-in-law, so I reckon he was the one had to be picked, seein' as he's family. But, you tell them nice folks up at Antelope Springs to be very careful when they're dealing with him, and not go signing over the family ranch."

Gib laughed. "Jane, sounds to me like you don't care all that much for Mr. Matthews."

"Let's just say that when he married Cindy Dempster, he come out a lot better on the deal than Cindy did."

Bill Pratt came out of the kitchen then, wiping his hands on the apron that swathed his ample belly. Coming over to Gib's table, he laughed softly and put his hand affectionately on Jane's arm. "Is she bendin' your ear, Gib? Woman, come on now, Gib ain't got time to be listenin' to all your palaver. He's got a stagecoach to drive."

"I was just telling him about—"

"I'm sure I know what you was tellin' him," Bill said. "Now, go on. Them muffins you started bakin' need you back in the kitchen."

"All right, all right," Jane replied with a long-suffering sigh. She started to walk away from the table, then she turned to smile back at Gib. "You be sure'n tell Madge I said hello, won't you?"

"I surely will," the driver promised.

"And you, Beans, you come again next time you're in Rock Creek."

"Yes, ma'am, I'll do that," Beans promised, still not looking up from his plate.

Bill Pratt watched his wife walk back to the

kitchen and then shook his head, apologizing, "I'm sorry about all her gabbing', Gib. But you know how women love to carry on."

"Oh, I didn't mind at all," Gib insisted. Keeping his voice low, he continued. "Fact is, that was real good information she give me 'bout Matthews, 'cause if someone is plannin' on carryin' a lot of money with 'em on board my stagecoach, why, I'd sure like to know somethin' about it. If we're goin' to be waylaid, I damn well want to know what it is we're bein' waylaid for." Gib stood, took a couple of coins from his pocket, then placed them on the table. "Here's for the supper for me an' my shotgun," he said. "And I'll be needin' a receipt if you don't mind."

"I don't mind at all. Was everything all right?"

"Real good," Gib replied. He looked at Beans and smiled. "And from the looks of that spankin'-clean plate, I don't think Beans had any complaints, either."

"It was real good," Beans agreed, standing as well. "Say, Gib, I almost forgot somethin' I'm supposed to take care of before we head out. I'll meet you over at the stage in plenty of time."

"Okay. Just don't make me have to wait none. The passengers get mighty upset if we ain't ready to go when we're supposed to."

"I'll be there," Beans promised. Nodding to

the restaurant owner, the shotgun guard turned to leave, pushing through the front door. Despite his size, or maybe because of it, his gait had a bit of a swagger as he hurried out on his short, bandy legs.

"That's sure a little feller there," Bill noted. "But judging from the scar that's decoratin' his face, I got me an idear that he ain't someone you'd be wantin' to get on your bad side."

"You've got that right," Gib replied.

"I don't believe I've seen him before. Has he been with you long?"

"No, he just started workin' with the company," Gib explained. "Truth is, I don't really know too much about him myself, including his real name. I'm pretty sure no mama would name her boy Beans."

Bill laughed. "Where'd he come from?" he asked.

"Don't know that, either," Gib admitted, rubbing his chin thoughtfully.

"You don't seem to know much about him a'tall."

"Well, I do know some about him," Gib defended. "He tended bar up in Antelope Springs for a while, worked as a hustler over to Soda Springs, deputied some up in Johnson County. And he worked as a cowboy."

"Ridin' shotgun is a pretty responsible job," Bill said. "You reckon he's up to it?"

"Well, he don't talk much when we're rollin', but he don't miss a thing on the trail. And when you get right down to it, what do you need to know to be a shotgun guard, anyway? All I really require is that he shows up on time, stays sober, and keeps his eyes open. He does all that just fine."

"We know he's got a good appetite, especially for such a little man," Bill observed, chuckling. He tore a piece of paper from a writing tablet, jotted down a figure, and signed it. "Here's your receipt," he said, handing the paper over to Gib.

"Thanks," the driver said, sticking it in his pocket. "The home office is real particular about this. Time was when I could just tell 'em what I spent for my meals, and they wouldn't say nothin'. But some folks along the line was beginning to take advantage of it. And besides that, prices is gettin' so high nowadays. I mean, who'd have ever thought it'd cost a fella twenty-five cents just to eat a meal?"

"You sayin' we overcharge in here?" Bill asked. It was a friendly challenge.

Smiling at the restaurant owner, Gib put on his hat. "It don't matter what it cost, this here is still the best food in all of Wyoming," he said. "I'll be seeing you on my next trip down."

"Stay out of trouble, Gib," Bill called to his best customer as he began clearing away the table.

*   *   *

Quince never thought he would see the day when he would welcome a plate of beans, but he would give anything for a plate of them now. He had killed and eaten a rabbit yesterday, but the best he had been able to manage so far today was some wild greens. And though the greens managed to fill the emptiness in his stomach and provided him, he supposed, with some nourishment, they had no flavoring of any kind, not even salt.

He wasn't exactly sure where he was, though he was drifting in a northerly direction on a trail that he supposed would eventually lead him to Antelope Springs.

The smart thing to do would be to head west, to California or Oregon. He could change his name and make a new life out there. No one would know him, and he doubted that any notice of his escape would go that far. On the other hand, nearly everyone in Antelope Springs would have heard of his escape by now and, if anyone up there saw him, they would recognize him immediately.

He argued with himself. Why go to Antelope Springs? There was nothing there for him now. His only family had been his brother, and now he was dead. The ranch he and his brother had worked so hard to build was gone, eaten up by legal fees and the taxes that couldn't be paid while he was in prison. The one girl that had ever really interested him had moved to Boston. And even if she hadn't, she would have nothing to do with him now. He was a fugitive. It made no difference that he was innocent of the crime which put him in jail in the first place. He was now an escaped convict, and that act alone made him a criminal.

On the other hand, he had some idea that he could prove his innocence. It all depended upon whether or not he could find Deekus Tombs and get him to confess that Quince and his brother had nothing to do with that bank holdup. It also depended upon him finding a lawman who would be sympathetic enough to his situation to give him an opportunity to prove his innocence. That man would be Will Jordan, the sheriff at Antelope Springs. Jordan had been the only person to believe him, and the only person to testify on his behalf.

As Quince trudged along, he remembered, vividly, the dark days of his trial.

The chief witness for the prosecution had been Grady Orr, the town blacksmith. Orr had been repairing the bell tower of the church on the day of the bank robbery, and because of his unique vantage point, was the prosecution's key witness.

"And now, Mr. Orr, I point to the defendant,

Quince Fremont, and ask if you have ever seen him before," the prosecutor asked.

"Yes, sir, I certainly have," Orr replied.

"Where did you see him?"

"Him and his brother was part of that bunch of cutthroat murderers and robbers that come into town to rob the bank."

"And you witnessed this?"

"Oh, yes, sir, I witnessed it real good."

"Where were you when you witnessed this heinous crime?"

"I was up in the bell tower," Orr answered.

"Please tell the jury what happened."

"Well, sir, when folks realized there was a bank robbery goin' on, they all armed themselves and commenced shooting. I remember thinking how much I wish I had my Winchester up there in the steeple with me, because I had the best view in town. But who woulda thought you'd need a Winchester in a church bell tower?"

"Yes, who indeed?" the prosecutor said. "Mr. Orr, would you tell us how it is that you happened to recognize this particular defendant as one of the cutthroat thieves?"

"Yes, sir. Well, this fella here"—Orr pointed to Quince—"and his brother was wearing shirts that was just alike. This here'n got his horse shot out from under him. So his brother goes over to the hitchin' rail and steals another horse."

"That would be the horse belonging to Win Sherman?"

"Yes, sir, that's the one."

"Then what happened?"

"Well, Sherman come out after him. He set a big store by that horse and he was tryin' to save 'im. But the next thing you know, Sherman got hisself shot at point-blank range. Even from where I was up in the bell tower, I could see that poor ol' Win was kilt, dead as a doornail."

"The defendant shot him?"

"Yes."

"No further questions, Your Honor."

The lawyer for the defense rose to question Orr. "Mr. Orr, you said the defendant got his horse shot from under him?"

"That's right."

"And his brother then got Mr. Sherman's horse, murdering Mr. Sherman in the process?"

"That's right, that's what happened."

"But you also said the defendant is the one who shot Win Sherman. Now, which is it?"

"I . . ." Orr hesitated. "That is . . . they was both wearing the same kind of shirt. Maybe I've got 'em mixed up. Yeah, that's it. Now that I think about it, it could be that the other fella was the one that got unseated, and this here one is the one who killed Win Sherman for his horse."

"But you really don't know which one it was, do you?"

"Objection, Your Honor. It really doesn't make any difference. A murder in the commission of a felony is murder in the first degree. Whether Quince Fremont or Cole Fremont pulled the trigger on poor Win Sherman, both are equally guilty."

"Your Honor, it *does* make a difference," the defense attorney quickly said. "I contend that Mr. Orr isn't identifying the men . . . he is identifying the shirts." The lawyer went over to the exhibit table and picked up the two plaid shirts that were being used as evidence. "We will stipulate that the shirts were in town on the day of the robbery. But neither Quince Fremont, nor his brother, were wearing them."

Quince's lawyer was good, and if reason and logic had prevailed over hotheaded temper and the need for revenge, he might have carried the day. After decimating the stories told by witnesses for the prosecution, he called only one witness for the defense. Sheriff Will Jordan.

"Sheriff Jordan, you have no legal jurisdiction in Theresa, is that right?" the defense counsel asked.

"That's right, I'm not a county sheriff, I'm a town sheriff for the town of Antelope Springs. And though I have tracked fugitives beyond the city limits, such authority is granted me only when I am in actual pursuit."

"Then may I ask why, if you have no jurisdiction here in Theresa, are you testifying in this trial?"

"Because I would not like to see the people of Theresa rush to judgment," Jordan replied. He turned in his chair, slightly, so he could address the jury.

"I've known Quince and Cole Fremont for a long time. They are decent, hard-working ranchers who have never violated any law. In fact, on a couple of occasions, they have acted as special deputies for me. They are well respected by everyone in Antelope Springs, so when I heard that they were accused of taking part in the bank robbery here in Theresa, I didn't believe it. And listening to the testimony given in this trial, I am more convinced than ever that Quince Fremont is innocent."

"Sheriff, would you tell how you have come to that decision?" the defense counsel asked.

"To begin with, the blacksmith says that either Quince or Cole Fremont rode out of town on Win Sherman's horse. But there are two pieces of evidence that contradict that. For example, when the posse came upon Quince and Cole Fremont, the horses the two men were riding were their own. They were identified as such by the brands they were wearing. In addition, I could personally identify Quince's horse."

"How is it that you can make this personal identification?" the defense counsel asked.

"Because I sold him that horse myself. I raised him from the time he was a colt," Will answered.

"Go on, Sheriff. You said there were other considerations that convince you of Mr. Fremont's innocence."

"Yes, sir. There is the question of the bullet that killed Win Sherman. The doctor said it was a 36-caliber ball. I know that both Quince and Cole packed forty-fours, and that's what they were carrying when the posse found them. And, finally, there are the plaid shirts Quince and Cole were supposed to be wearing. But as I explained, I've known Quince and his brother for a very long time, and I never saw those shirts before."

"Thank you, Sheriff Jordan. Your witness, counselor," the defense attorney said to the prosecutor.

The prosecutor was an overweight, red-faced, bald-headed man wearing a three-piece suit. A gold watch chain spanned his considerable girth, and he played with it for a moment as he approached the jury box. He turned toward Will Jordan.

"Mr. Jordan," he began, purposely omitting the use of the term "sheriff." "Were you in Theresa on the day of the bank robbery?"

"No, I wasn't."

"Then your status as witness for the defense is that of character witness, is that right?"

Jordan cleared his throat. "I suppose so."

"Oh, there's no suppose to it, Mr. Jordan," the prosecutor said. "The truth is, the jury has been told what happened in Theresa by eyewitnesses, people who were on the scene and who saw Quince Fremont and his brother robbing and killing. You, on the other hand, have no first-hand knowledge of the event. You have only your theory of what happened."

"I prefer to call it logic," Jordan replied.

"Well, sir, let's just take a closer look at your logic," the prosecutor suggested. "You say you recognized the mounts the Fremont brothers were riding as being their own when the posse found them. On the surface that might lead a person to wonder, then, what happened to Win Sherman's horse. But let me ask you this: Would it not make sense for them to keep their horses out of harm's way until after the foul deed was done? Then it would be a simple matter of abandoning the horses they used for the robbery—including Win Sherman's horse—so they could make their escape on fresh mounts? The same holds true with the guns. Use revolvers of one caliber while committing the robbery, then exchange them for others, so that the caliber of the bullets at the scene of the crime would not match the caliber of the bullets in the guns they were carrying. And, indeed, Mr. Jordan, if the jury followed your logic, then evil subterfuge would succeed. And as for the shirts? Well, men who are planning to rob a bank would hardly be expected to wear the same shirt in town that they planned to use during a bank robbery, would they?

"Gentlemen of the jury, do not be misled by a smart lawyer's tricks. Quince Fremont is guilty as sin. Nearly everyone in this town saw him in the midst of the killing frenzy that took place here less than six weeks ago. I ask you to find him guilty of armed robbery and murder. And I ask you to instruct the judge to assess the penalty of death by hanging."

The prosecutor prevailed, at least to the degree of winning a conviction. But the jury, perhaps influenced in some degree due to Will Jordan's testimony, and the fact that no eyewitness could positively identify Quince as the one who pulled the trigger, threw out the charge of murder. As a result, Quince went to prison, but he did not go to the gallows.

Seeing a flat rock, Quince sat down for a short breather. He thought of the line he had once heard while attending a production of Shakespeare. "A horse, a horse, my kingdom for a horse."

Well, Quince didn't have a kingdom, but he

surely could have used a horse about then. He took his boots off and examined his feet for blisters.

The rattle of a snake made his hair stand on end. Looking slowly to his left, he saw that the rattler was coiled within striking distance, its tail shaking wildly. If he tried to get up, the snake would get him before he could get away. He had only one option, and he played it, hoping that the cowboy he took the gun from had kept it in good working condition.

Quince drew and fired just as the snake started its strike. The bullet smashed through the snake's open mouth, blowing out the back of its head.

Quince grabbed the still twitching body of the dead snake and threw it as far as he could. He shuddered involuntarily and the hair on the back of his neck stood on end as he thought about what could have happened.

"Wait a minute!" he said aloud. "What the hell am I thinking?" He laughed and walked toward the area where he had flung the serpent's body. "Mr. Snake, you are going to be my lunch."

Chapter Seven

As the stagecoach driver walked across the street, he saw that the luggage was already loaded. He was grateful that he would not have to load it himself.

"We got you all loaded, Mr. Crabtree, 'ceptin' for the passengers," one of the hostlers said.

"Thanks, boys," Gib answered. "I appreciate that a lot. I think I'm gettin' too old to haul them trunks up top."

"You ain't old, Mr. Crabtree. You just ripe," one of the hostlers said, and the other laughed at the joke.

Gib saw a little cluster of people standing on the platform near the stagecoach. These, he figured, would be the passengers for Antelope Springs. One of them was a relatively small man who held a black satchel to his chest and paced back and forth nervously. From the way he was clutching it so possessively, Gib figured this had to be the banker who was responsible for the money shipment. Laughing to himself, the driver thought that the banker was so small that anybody who wanted it could probably jerk the bag away from him, no matter how tightly he held on to it.

He saw the little man step away from the others and walk toward him. "I am Ethan Matthews, vice president of the Rock Creek Bank," he said.

"Mr. Matthews," Gib replied, touching the brim of his cap in a greeting.

"We have been waiting for you," the little banker remarked petulantly. "Departure time on the schedule board is nine o'clock." He pulled out his pocket watch and looked at it. "As it lacks only five minutes of nine, and we are all here, I think we should go right now."

Gib pulled the watch from his pocket and looked at it. "We will leave by my watch, and according to my chronometer we have eight minutes yet."

"I believe I told you who I was?"

"Matthews, I think you said."

Matthews seemed to pull himself together for a moment, almost as if he were preening. He cleared his throat. "Perhaps you should also know I am a person of no small importance in this town. I'm not used to waiting."

"Well, whether you are used to it or not, we ain't goin' nowhere till Mr. Evans gets here."

"Mr. Evans? I don't understand. Who is Evans and why should we wait for him?"

"He is our shotgun guard."

"I see. And just where might Mr. Evans be?"

"I'm not sure."

"You're not sure," Matthews said. He crossed his arms against his chest and began tapping his foot impatiently on the ground. He looked toward the other passengers. "It is time to leave, his guard is not here, and he's not sure where he is," he said in an agitated voice.

"All I know is, he said he had to run an errand. If he's a minute or two late, it ain't goin' to hurt nothin'," the driver said.

"No doubt that is the way you look at it," Matthews said. "On the other hand, with such an irresponsible guard and a lackadaisical driver, I suppose we will be lucky if we get there at all."

"You know, Mr. Matthews, I have the authority to refuse passage to anyone I think might be a troublemaker," Gib said. "Maybe you would like to find some other way to Antelope Springs."

"You know there isn't another way," Matthews replied in a blustering voice.

"Well, now, that's true, isn't it?" Gib replied easily. "So I reckon that means if you are going to ride with me you're going to have to complain a mite less."

With a frustrated clearing of his throat, Matthews walked back over to join the other passengers.

"Folks, we'll be leavin' in just a few minutes," Gib said to the passengers. "If you got any last-minute thing to take care of, best you get it done." He nodded toward the two outhouses which sat a short distance away from the depot.

"Lucy, do you need to visit the outhouse before we leave?" Kate asked.

"No, Mama."

Gib had started toward the front of the coach, but when he recognized the woman's voice, he turned back quickly, surprised to see that one of his passengers was Kate O'Leary. He smiled broadly and walked over to her. "Mrs. O'Leary, if you ain't a sight for sore eyes. I thought we'd lost you to some place back East. Are you going up to Antelope Springs?"

"I sure am."

"Well, now, that's really fine news," Gib said. "You know, Madge is going to be real happy to see you again. You always was special to her. How long will you be visitin'?"

"I'm not visiting, Mr. Crabtree. Lucy and I are moving back home. We didn't care much for Philadelphia, so I'm going to reopen the hotel and live in Antelope Springs."

"You don't say! Why, that's wonderful!" Gib smiled down at Lucy. "And I'll tell you somebody else who's going to be real happy to hear this," he said to the little girl. "Lucy, would you believe that since you left, my little granddaughter hasn't been able to find herself another best friend?"

"I can be her best friend again?" Lucy asked, smiling brightly.

"Sure now, and I know she'd be all for that."

Rachel Kincaid stepped forward. "Hello, Mr. Crabtree. Do you remember me?"

Gib studied the beautiful young woman who spoke to him. "Ah, Rachel, girl, you are even more beautiful now than you was when you left us," he said. "City life sure seems to have agreed with you. Your pa told me you was goin' to be on this train. He and your ma are really lookin' forward to your comin' back. What a welcome this coach will get when we pull into Antelope in a couple of days. Two of the prettiest women the town ever produced, comin' back home."

"Yes, well, unlike Mrs. O'Leary, I'm not coming back to stay," Rachel responded. "You see, the truth is that city life agrees with me a lot more than life out here. So I'm going to stay in Wyoming only so long as it takes to convince Ma and Pa to sell the ranch and move East."

"Well, now, why in heaven's name would you want to do a thing like that?" Gib asked, surprised by her suggestion.

"Because, unlike everyone in this godforsaken place, the people back East live like human beings." As if to make her case, she looked pointedly at the unpainted outhouses.

"Oh, I see," Gib said. He stroked his long mustache as he studied her. "Well, I'm just real sorry you feel that way, Rachel. And as far as you talkin' your folks into leavin' us out here, well, I'm afraid I can't wish you much success with that. You see, ever'one up in Antelope Springs sort of regards your ma and pa with a lot of affection, and I don't think there's anyone who would like to see 'em just up an' leave."

Suddenly Ethan Matthews stepped in front of Gib Crabtree and, ignoring Rachel Kincaid, pointed across the street. "I hate to interrupt old home week, driver, but would that be the man we are waiting for?" he asked.

"Yes, it is," Gib replied.

"Then I see no reason for further delay. Kindly get this vehicle underway at once," Matthews fumed.

"That's just what I plan to do, mister," Gib said with a patronizing smirk on his face. He looked back at the others who were waiting to board the stage. "All right, folks, if you're all ready, climb aboard and I'll see if I can get this stubborn team of ornery cayuses to pull us."

While the driver stood watching, the two women and the young girl boarded, then Ethan

Matthews began to climb inside. Beans reached the stagecoach just as Will Jordan did. The driver greeted his shotgun guard, then he turned to the lawman, saying softly, "Sheriff, I'm glad you're riding with us. It turns out one of our passengers is carrying a lot of money on this trip, so it'll be good to have extra protection."

Will stopped in his tracks and stared at Gib Crabtree. "Now, how in Sam Hill did you know about the money?" he asked, clearly taken aback. "It was supposed to be kept secret."

"Hell, Sheriff, it's our business to know," Beans replied, answering for Gib.

Damon Parker, who was waiting to board the stage just behind the sheriff, said, "Judging from the way that little gentleman is gripping his black bag, I'd say that's where the money is." He pointed to Ethan Matthews, and the little black satchel he was holding with both arms.

The lawman gaped at Damon. "And you not only know about the money, you know who has it. How in blazes has everyone found out about this? Is there a big sign on the side of the coach?" Jordan asked sarcastically.

Smiling, Damon lay his finger alongside his nose. "Let's just say it is a matter of professionalism," he said. "I'm a gambler, you see, and money is my stock-in-trade. I can smell it."

The gambler and the lawman got into the

coach. Jordan, Matthews, and Damon settled down in the rear-facing seat, while Kate, Lucy, and Rachel sat in the forward-facing one. The girl sat between the two women, lying with her head in her mother's lap and her feet resting on Rachel's knees. The expression on her face bespoke her discomfort.

However, when Damon settled into his seat, the look on the little girl's face changed to amazement. "Mister," she asked quietly, "can you *really* smell money?"

Damon laughed heartily. "Well, now, missy, it could be that I overstated my talent just a bit. I wouldn't actually want to be put to the test."

"You mean you *can't* smell money?" Lucy asked, her disappointment clearly evident.

"I'm afraid not."

Lucy smiled. "Well, if you can't really smell money, why did you say you could? That's telling a fib."

"Lucy!" Kate scolded, unable to keep the laugh out of her voice. Putting a finger to her daughter's lips she shook her head. "Hush, now. It's just an expression, that's all. Now you apologize."

"No apology necessary," Damon said quickly.

The child looked first at her mother and then at Damon. "I'm sorry," she said.

"That's quite all right, young lady. I shouldn't have said something that would confuse you."

"Folks," Gib Crabtree announced as he placed his hand on the door. "I hope you kept out somethin' warm to wear at night. It's mild enough in the daytime, but this bein' early spring an' all, why, come dark you're goin' to think you're in the dead of winter. There's still ice in the cricks at night, and likely there will be some snow on the ground in the higher elevations."

Murmurs of assurance rose from the passengers, then Gib closed and latched the door and climbed up to the driver's box. Beans was already on top, sitting at his place on the seat with a rifle cradled across his lap. Settling in beside him, Gib released the brake and then took the whip from its holder and popped it over the team's heads. The coach immediately started forward, and within minutes it rolled down the main street of Rock Creek, soon reaching the outskirts of town.

As the stagecoach rolled north, Damon Parker leaned his head back against the seat. He closed his eyes and listened as Rachel Kincaid began telling Kate O'Leary a story about an adventure she had experienced while she was in Boston. Soon the gambler dozed off, and he found himself dreaming a dream he had had many times before. Coincidentally, the dream concerned a young woman about the same age as Rachel, and it took place in Boston. Damon was able to anticipate with great trepidation the terrible sequence of events as they unfolded in his recurring dream, although he was forced each time to relive the images as if he were viewing them for the first time.

It always started the same way: He was in a room near the Boston harbor, and he could hear a bell clanging in a nearby buoy, its syncopated ringing sounding a repeated warning. The traffic outside was muted by the fog, and even the clip-clopping of horses' hooves on the cobblestones was barely audible. Inside the brightly lit room was a young woman who was clearly frightened, but Damon was telling her that she had absolutely nothing to fear.

"I make you a solemn promise that everything will be just fine, Deborah," he reassured the beautiful brunette in his dream. "I give you my guarantee."

"And if it isn't all right?" the woman asked, a note of irony in her voice. "How will I be able to call in the guarantee?"

In his dream, the images would suddenly shift in time and space, Damon would be shivering and sweating at the same time, finding himself looking down at a woman's bloody, lifeless body. His hands would be covered with the woman's blood as he held them up in front of his face and cried out in agony, "No . . . no! My God, what have I done?"

"Mr. Parker? Mr. Parker, wake up!" a woman's voice called, wrenching Damon from his troubled sleep.

Opening his eyes, the gambler sat up with a start, realizing then that he was a passenger in a stagecoach two thousand miles from Boston. His cold, shivering hands were raised in front of him and all the passengers were staring at him. The women had expressions of concern and compassion on their faces, while the men were merely curious.

"Mr. Parker?" Kate asked again. "Are you all right?"

Damon swallowed, then nodded, forcing himself to smile. "Mrs. O'Leary . . . indeed, all of you, I am fine. It was merely a bad dream."

"You're sure you are all right?" Kate O'Leary pressed.

"Yes, quite," Damon murmured. "There is no need for concern. As I said, it was just a bad dream."

Leaning back against the seat, Damon stared out the window, trying as hard as he could to blot out the painful images that would burn forever in his memory.

Chapter Eight

There were no street lamps in the little hamlet of Millersburg. It was much too small for such civilized amenities. The lights that the stage-coach passengers had seen from a distance as they followed the switchback road down the mountain had come from the handful of build-ings: a hotel and restaurant, a general store, a saloon, and a livery stable that also served as the stage station. In addition to the five commercial buildings, there were perhaps a dozen houses.

The coach clattered into town, the light from its twin kerosene sidelights illuminating the dusty street. Finally it drew to a stop in front of the livery stable.

"Lucy, wake up, honey, we're going to spend the night here," Kate said.

Lucy sat up and rubbed her eyes. "Where are we, Mama?" she asked, her voice slurring with sleep.

"We're in Millersburg," Kate answered. Pointing through the window, she explained, "We're going to go across the street and get a room in that hotel over there."

"Kate, I can go on ahead and get our rooms," Rachel offered.

"Thank you, I'd appreciate that," Kate answered. Then she looked down at Lucy. "Are you hungry, dear? What would you like for supper?"

"I don't feel like eating, Mama," Lucy groaned. "My stomach is hurting real bad."

"It's still hurting? Oh, my, I hoped it would have quit by now."

Damon Parker stepped out of the coach first, and helped Rachel down before reaching for Lucy. As he gently lifted her, she winced.

"I'm sorry, honey," Damon said kindly. "I sure didn't mean to hurt you."

"That's all right," Lucy replied. "I think it just hurts now because I'm tired from sleeping." Looking at her mother she asked, "Mama, do I have to go to bed right away?"

"Tired from sleeping, huh?" Kate repeated with a laugh. "Well, I'm glad to hear that. You can't be feeling too poorly if you're wanting to stay up."

Gib Crabtree and Beans Evans climbed down from the top of the coach and stretched while a couple of hostlers hurried out to unharness the team and lead them off for food and water. Ethan

Matthews then stepped out of the stagecoach and immediately crossed the street. He was followed by Will Jordan, who stood with the others. The men watched Matthews walk quickly toward the hotel, hurrying along behind Kate and Lucy.

"Look at how tight that little feller is holdin' that bag. Wouldn't you hate to try and grab it away from him?" Gib asked with a chuckle. "He'd just give you the fight of your life."

The others laughed with him.

"Well, I for one, hope nobody tries to take it," Will said. "I'm getting paid extra to watch over him, and I'd like nothing better than for this trip to be peaceable!"

From the saloon across the way came a woman's high-pitched shriek, followed by the laughter of a dozen or more men. After that a piano began playing, and the notes spilled through the batwing doors into the street. One cowboy lurched out of the saloon and started up the boardwalk away from the coach, while two others seemed to materialize out of the darkness in front of the saloon, pushing their way through the doors to go inside. The North Star Saloon was the most brightly lit building in town, and it seemed to draw the cowboys to its glow with the same magnetism with which the gleaming kerosene lanterns here and there were drawing fluttering moths.

"Gib, do you stay in the hotel when you spend the night in this town?" Jordan asked.

"No," the driver answered. He stretched and yawned and then scratched his head, ruffling his gray hair. "The company keeps a room for me and my shotgun guard in the back of the livery. Sometimes, though, if we happen to meet a coach goin' the other way, and the other driver and shotgun is usin' the room, why, I'll just slide the seats together in the coach and stay in there. It makes up into a fine bed if there ain't no more'n two or three tryin' to use it."

"You planning on doing that tonight?"

"Well, I'd planned on staying in the room tonight. Why? You want to use the coach? You're welcome to it, if you want it."

"Thanks. Maybe I'll just take you up on it."

"Sheriff, if you don't mind some company, I'd like to stay in the coach with you," Damon said. He looked over toward the North Star Saloon, adding, "I'd rather spend my money on drink than sleep anytime."

Jordan laughed. "Can't say as I blame you. I could use a little snort myself. What say we mosey on over there and have a couple?"

Rachel Kincaid had managed to get adjoining rooms for herself and the O'Learys. Stopping first in the hotel dining room, the three weary travelers ate supper, then went upstairs to their rooms on the second floor.

With the door between the rooms standing ajar, Rachel washed her face and hands at the basin on the table in her room, while in the next room Kate sat on the edge of the bed, looking after her daughter. Lucy had barely touched her supper, and now she was complaining that her stomach was hurting more than ever.

"You know, Rachel," Kate called, "I'm beginning to be worried about her. It isn't at all like her to be sick like this, and if it had simply been train sickness or something she ate earlier, I should think it would be over by now."

Putting down the towel, Rachel fastened the several buttons she had opened on the neck of her dress, and walked into the adjoining room. She leaned over Lucy, feeling her face and then remarked softly to Kate. "I'd say she has a slight fever. Tell you what—why don't I go downstairs and ask if there's a doctor in town? If there is, I'll send for him then come right back."

"Oh, would you? I'd be very grateful," Kate breathed, her face pale with worry.

Rachel hurried down the stairs and then across the worn, red-carpeted lobby to the front desk. The middle-aged clerk was reading a newspaper by the lamp on his desk, and he laid the paper aside and began preening his thick dark mustache as the beautiful young woman approached.

"Well, now, little lady," the clerk mumbled, "what can I do for you?"

"Is there a doctor in this town?"

"Well, there is Doc Urban," the clerk said. "Some folks don't think too highly of him, but if you'd like, I could run him down for you."

"Thank you, but the doctor isn't for me," Rachel explained. "I want him for my friend's little girl. The child is having terrible stomach pains."

"The little girl, huh? Well, I reckon whatever ails the girl won't tax Doc's skills none. I'll go get hold of him and send him on up to the girl's room."

"Thank you," Rachel replied. "The room number is—"

"We ain't all that full, miss, that I don't know where you are," the clerk said, smiling easily. "You're in 204, and the girl and her mama are in 202. Is that right?"

"Yes. How long do you think before the doctor will get here?"

"Very soon, I would think. He's prob'ly just over to the saloon, gettin' himself a drink or two. He's purt' near always there this time of night."

"Thank you very much for your kindness," Rachel said, giving the clerk a sweet smile.

Rachel started back up the stairs, and as she did so, Ethan Matthews was coming down. Matthews put up his hand, stopping her progress. He took a long, slow, appraising look at Rachel, examining her from head to toe with such unabashed intensity that it almost made her feel as if he were undressing her.

"I was wondering if, uh, perhaps, we might have a drink together?" he asked.

The question surprised Rachel. "A drink? I'm afraid not. Thank you for asking, but I don't imbibe."

"I see," Matthews mumbled. "Well," he went on, putting his hand on her forearm, "I want you to know that if there is anything I can do for you, you'll find me just a few rooms down from your own." His hand began moving up and down, caressing her arm.

"Thank you," Rachel responded coolly, pulling away resolutely. "I'm sure I'll be able to handle everything just fine."

She turned, about to continue on up the stairs, but Matthews continued talking. "I listened with pleasure to your stories about Boston," Matthews said. "It must be a wonderful place."

"Yes, I liked it."

"I'm sure a young woman such as yourself could have a very pleasant time in a city like Boston."

"Yes, I suppose so," Rachel replied. She didn't

like the conversation, and she did not like the salacious gleam in the clerk's eyes.

"And if a young woman . . . say a very beautiful young woman such as yourself . . . were to play her cards right with a man with a very bright future . . . say, someone like me . . . then she might find the city even more enjoyable, don't you agree?" He put his hand back on her arm.

"A woman like me with a man like you?" Rachel snapped. "That could never be, Mr. Matthews."

Matthews's face grew dark, and the fingers of his gently caressing hand suddenly clamped down on her arm. "And what is wrong with a man like me?" he asked, his voice threatening. "Are you saying that I am not good enough for you?"

"No, Mr. Matthews. But I was told that you are married," Rachel replied easily. "And now, would you please let go of my arm? You are hurting me."

For a moment, Matthews acted almost as if he was astonished by his own behavior and he released his grip instantly, as if he had grabbed a hot iron. "Yes, yes, of course. Please forgive me," he muttered. He smiled. "You are right of course. I am married, and that's why I meant nothing . . . improper by my conversation. I was just suggesting that the time may well come when you have need of a friend. And, should that time come, I am offering myself in that capacity."

"Thank you, Mr. Matthews. I shall keep your offer in mind," Rachel said. "And now, if you will excuse me, I really must go see what I can do for Mrs. O'Leary." Without giving him time to respond, she turned and hurried up the stairs.

A few minutes after Rachel had returned to Kate's room, a knock sounded on the door. Rachel opened it, and what greeted her was one of the most unimpressive figures of a man she had ever seen. A short, fat, totally disreputable-looking man stood there. His jacket and shirt-front were dotted with dozens of unidentifiable stains, and he had his hand stuck in between the buttons of his shirt, scratching his belly. Even from here, she could smell his body odor. She took a step back from the door.

"You sent for a doctor?" the man asked. He belched.

"I did. Is he on his way?"

"On his way, madam?" the man replied. He held his hand up, his index finger pointing toward the ceiling. "I am he," he said.

The man had obviously been drinking, and though he didn't appear to be drunk, the strong smell of alcohol on his breath competed with his body odor.

"Where is the child?" the doctor asked.

"She's here, Doctor," Kate called from farther back in the room. She was sitting on the edge of the bed, holding a damp cloth to Lucy's forehead. "There's something terribly wrong with her. I think it's far more than a simple stomachache."

"I see, madam," the doctor said haughtily. "And you are a doctor, of course?"

"What?" Kate asked in surprise. "No, of course not."

"Then kindly leave the diagnosis to me," Dr. Urban said, moving over to the bed.

Rachel watched him warily. In addition to being short, fat, and filthy, his skin was red and blotchy. In fact he had such an altogether unhealthy appearance that Rachel thought her first impression—that of his being a messenger from the saloon who normally swept floors and emptied spittoons—was unfair to floor sweepers and spittoon tenders.

Doctor Urban set his bag down on the dresser, opened it, and took out a flat stick. Putting the stick on Lucy's tongue, he ordered her to say "ah."

As the doctor examined her, he pushed the tongue depressor so far down into the child's throat that Lucy gagged and then began crying.

"Young lady, it's hard to look you over if you are going to be such a crybaby," the physician mocked.

"Doctor, please," Kate complained, "she's

only seven years old and she isn't feeling well. And frankly, you aren't being very gentle with that stick."

"Madam, if you don't like the way I'm doctoring, you can always get another one," Urban rejoined. He put the stick back in his bag, and Rachel wondered if that meant he planned to use it with another patient at some time in the future. Then, with a gasp, she wondered if it had been used before.

"Is there another doctor in this town?" Kate asked coolly.

"Not for fifty miles, madam," Urban replied.

"Then we obviously can't get another one, can we?"

"Nope."

The doctor took a look at each of Lucy's eyes, and then measured her pulse. Rachel glanced at Kate, and when their eyes met, they exchanged a look that said Urban seemed to be acting professionally enough. Finally he completed his examination and stood up.

"Well, you can put your mind to rest, madam," he said to Kate. "Your daughter doesn't seem to have anything seriously wrong with her."

"Thank God," Kate responded with a sigh.

"In fact, she's not suffering from any of the usual maladies that I can see. Perhaps the travel has made her somewhat irregular. That would

give her a stomachache, sure as shootin'. I'll pre-
pare a purgative for her. That'll clean her out
well enough, and she shouldn't have any more
problems. That'll cost you twenty-five cents. Do
you want it?"

"Yes, of course, if that's what it takes to get
her well," Kate replied.

Doctor Urban looked across the room at the
water pitcher. "Any water left in that jug over
there, girl?" he asked Rachel.

"Yes."

Urban took a small, brown bottle from his bag
and handed it to her. "Fill this bottle to about
here," he said, indicating with his finger.

Rachel did as directed and then handed the
bottle back. The physician rummaged through
his medical bag and finally extracted an enve-
lope. Opening it, he poured some white powder
into the bottle, stoppered it, gave it a good
shake, and then handed it over to Kate.

"You go ahead and give her a good dose of
it now, and then give her another just before she
goes to sleep. Keep on givin' it to her until she
quits complainin'." Picking up his bag, the doctor said, "That'll be a dollar for my services."

Kate walked to the dresser to her reticule,
reached into it and extracted a silver dollar.
Handing it to the physician, she told him, "I
really appreciate your coming over to the hotel
to see her at this time of night, Doctor. And I

am very glad that she isn't suffering from anything serious."

"Nothin' serious at all, madam," he assured her. Nodding to each of the women, he left the room on slightly unsteady feet.

Chapter Nine

Over at the North Star Saloon, the piano player was grinding out "Buffalo Gals." One of the bar girls was leaning on the back of the piano, singing along off-key. She was the only one paying any attention to the music. At all the other tables as well as at the bar, the cowboys and other patrons were engaged in so many loud, animated conversations that the piano and singer were barely audible.

Will Jordan and Damon Parker were at a table near the bar. The lawman took a swallow of his beer and studied the gambler over the rim of his glass. "You're the fellow they run out of Rock Creek, aren't you?"

"Well, I prefer to think of it as a going-away committee wanted to see me to the stage and tell me good-bye."

Jordan laughed. "I'll give you this, you have a sense of humor." He was quiet for a moment. "So now you are coming to my town?"

"That is my plan," Damon answered.

"Do you cheat at cards, Mr. Parker?" Jordan asked bluntly, his clear blue eyes staring intently across the table.

"No, I don't, Sheriff. Did the sheriff in Rock Creek accuse me of cheating?"

"Not exactly," Jordan replied. He licked the beer foam from his upper lip and then continued. "What he said was, you are so damn good that you win all the time. And he doesn't understand how anyone can do that without cheating, though he was quick to admit that no one has caught you cheating."

"That's because I don't. Never have, never will."

"Uh-huh," Jordan said.

Damon chuckled. "You don't believe me?"

"I don't know," Jordan admitted. "If you don't cheat, I would be interested in knowing how you can win so often. Do you have some sort of system?"

"Sheriff, have you ever heard the expression, 'In the world of the blind, a one-eyed man is king'?"

"No, I can't say as I have," Jordan replied. He shifted his weight in the chair, then chuckled. "But it's a pretty good expression," he said. "I can see how that would be the case."

"Well, you are looking at living proof of that old chestnut," Damon said. "You see, most men who play poker, play it with their heart and their temper. But most of all, they play it with their pride. That leaves them very vulnerable."

"How do you play poker?"

Damon touched the side of his head with his finger. "I play with my brain," he explained. "And since I am usually the only one using his brain, that makes me the one-eyed man in the world of the blind."

Jordan laughed. "I don't know as a person could argue with that," he said.

"You would think that, wouldn't you?" Damon replied pensively. "Unfortunately, a lot of people have argued with it. Truth to tell, Sheriff, there isn't one town along the Union Pacific that would welcome me back."

"I didn't figure Rock Creek was the first town that ever asked you to leave," Jordan said. Leaning forward again, he took another swallow of his beer, finishing it. Putting the empty glass down, he wiped the back of his hand across his mouth before speaking. "But I'll make you this promise. If you aren't cheating, you won't be run out of my town. Antelope Springs always has room for an honest man, regardless of how he makes his living."

"Well, I appreciate that, Sheriff," Damon replied. "I really do."

Suddenly there was a loud burst of laughter from the bar, and both men looked toward the source. A short, fat man with a red face and big nose was the center of attention.

"Doc, you was in here tryin' to borrow the cost of another drink not more'n a half hour ago," somebody said. "And now you got a whole dollar to spend. How'd you come by it?"

"I did a bit of doctorin' on that kid that come in on the stage tonight," Urban answered. He put the dollar on the bar and watched attentively as the bartender filled a large glass with whiskey. Lifting his glass to his nose, he inhaled the aroma and then sighed with satisfaction just before he tossed the drink down.

"Ah," he breathed after a moment. "That was good, sir." He snickered, adding, "A damn sight tastier than the purgative I administered to that kid, I'd wager." Wordlessly, he held his glass out for more whiskey.

"What was wrong with the kid?" the bartender asked as he poured another drink.

The doctor laughed. "She was complaining of a stomachache. But if you ask me, she's just a whiner who's been mollycoddled by an overprotective mother. There's nothing wrong with her that a hand applied briskly to her little butt wouldn't cure. And, in about seven more years, I'd wager there will be plenty of men willing to take on that job, if you know what I mean," he added with a sly wink.

Those around the doctor exploded in ribald

laughter as Urban held out his glass yet again and then tossed down a third whiskey as quickly as he had the first two.

Overhearing the conversation, Damon turned away in disgust and stared into his beer with an angry expression on his face. "Somebody needs to take that gentleman out to the barn and teach him a few manners," he grumbled.

Jordan nodded. "I know what you mean," he replied. "When you share a long trip like this, the passengers begin to belong to one another, like cowboys working on the same spread. If an outsider says something about one of us, they are talking about all of us."

"That's true," Damon replied. "But it's much more than that. That man is a doctor . . . or at least, he is supposed to be one. He should show more compassion for his patient. The cardinal rule of a doctor is, 'First, do no harm.' For that man to administer a purgative without knowing what is wrong with Lucy is practically criminal."

Suddenly the town doctor shouted, "I tell you this, boys, I would change places with that little girl in a heartbeat, just to have that good-looking woman caring for me. Matter of fact, I don't think there's anything wrong with the kid . . . it's her pretty mama who's ailin'. And if they was to stay here for a while, I think I could come up with just the curative prescription for her. Me!"

Damon slammed his glass on the table and started to rise, his dark eyes flashing. Jordan quickly reached across the table and grabbed his forearm, but the gambler shook off his restraining hand, saying, "I think this so-called doctor needs curing of his ill-mannered, boorish behavior."

"Are you sure you want to start with him?" the lawman asked, keeping his voice low. "He's got a lot of friends, and they may well back him up."

"That's a chance I'll just have to take," Damon muttered. His handsome face stiff with anger, he strode up to the doctor's table and stood over him, glaring at him but saying nothing.

Urban finally looked up with watery eyes and asked in a besotted voice, "Something I can do for you, mister?"

"Yes," Damon replied coldly. "You can stop impugning Mrs. O'Leary."

"Mrs. O'Leary?" The physician's face was puzzled. "Oh! You mean that little girl's good-lookin' mama. Well, I mean no evil. What is she to you?"

"A friend, and I won't tolerate ungentlemanly conversation around or about her."

"I merely made the observation that she is overly protective of her daughter."

"It is my opinion that the little girl is quite ill."

"Oh? And on what do you base this diagnosis, *Doctor*?" Urban asked sarcastically, coming down hard on the last two words.

"She has been having rather severe abdominal pain, which appears to be more marked on the right side. Did you check for any abdominal swelling?"

"Who are you?" Urban asked.

"I told you, I'm a friend."

"Well . . . friend . . . the little girl has been traveling for some time, is that correct? First by train, and then by coach?"

"Yes."

"It has been my observation that such lengthy periods of travel can often bring about irregularity, especially in those who are somewhat frail. The little girl is suffering from nothing more than constipation, for which I have prescribed a cure."

"I don't think you have done a thorough enough examination to come to such a conclusion," Damon said.

Dr. Urban ran his hand through his hair and sighed. "Look, I apologize for the remarks I made about Mrs. O'Leary earlier. You are right, they were vulgar and uncalled for. And I may be an alcoholic, and a boor, but I am, above all, a doctor who believes in the Hippocratic oath. I would never knowingly do harm to a patient. You seem to be a learned man, so I ask you—

is it not possible that a person who has suffered from several days of irregularity would present the same symptoms as this young girl?"

"Yes, it's quite possible. But I don't think that would be the only thing that could cause this."

"Perhaps not, but it is the most logical thing," Urban said. "So until, or unless, another doctor overrides my prescription, she will be treated in accordance with my diagnosis."

"I accept your apology," Damon said. He returned to the table he had been sharing with Jordan.

"What do you think?" Jordan asked. "Does he know what he is doing?"

"I pray that he does," Damon said.

As if in a conscious effort to modulate the mood of the patrons, the piano player stopped playing the almost raucous swinging tunes and took a guitar case down from the top of the piano. The case was battered and scarred, but the guitar itself was exquisitely beautiful. The box was cherry red, giving way to a soft yellow. The way the piano player was holding it with such tender care showed that his true love was for this instrument, not for the gaudy piano. He tilted his head, then began playing.

"It's all right, he just quit playin' the piano and started playin' the guitar. There's still music downstairs," Felton Pogue said. He had opened the door just wide enough to listen to the ambient sounds from the saloon below.

From behind him, on a musk-scented bed, a naked woman laughed.

"You're a funny one," she said. "I've never been with a man who had to have music playing while he was sportin' with a woman."

"I don't need music," Felton said, turning to look back at her.

"Oh? You sure jumped out of bed fast enough when the piano stopped playing."

"I thought something was happening downstairs."

"Well, honey, I hope so," the woman replied in a low, throaty voice. "'Cause it sure as hell ain't happenin' up here."

"You don't understand," Felton said. "A man in my business has to be real careful. I need to know what's goin' on around me all the time."

"And just what is your business?"

Felton smiled audaciously. "I rob banks," he said matter-of-factly.

Back in the hotel, Kate and Rachel were discussing their journey. They were speaking softly, for Lucy had finally fallen into a restless sleep on the bed behind them.

"I sure will be glad when we get there," Kate

said. "Maybe a few days of rest is all Lucy needs. It seems as if we've been traveling forever."

"Doesn't it, though?" Rachel replied.

Kate laughed. "And yet, it's only been a few days since Lucy and I stepped onto the train in Philadelphia. When I think of all the people who made this long journey before the railroad was built, why, it makes me positively ashamed for feeling sorry for myself."

"I know," Rachel said. "My mother and father came out West on a wagon train. They could hardly wait to get out here, but I can hardly wait to go back East."

Kate smiled. "Oh, now, Rachel, I wouldn't be so quick to make up my mind if I were you. Maybe you'll surprise yourself and decide this is where you belong. After all, your roots are here, aren't they? Surely there are some things you can remember with fondness."

"Oh, yes," Rachel admitted. "Seeing that sunrise this morning reminded me of all the sunrises and sunsets I used to enjoy on the ranch. And I remember the way the bighorn sheep would play on the sides of the mountains and the sounds their hooves would make, clattering against the rocks when they would break into a run." A faraway look came into her eyes, and she continued, "I always loved hearing the cattle low in the evening, when the cows would start calling out to their calves. And I confess that I miss being able to ride a horse . . . I don't mean ride a horse sidesaddle in a city park while wearing some stylish riding habit. I mean really ride like the wind, dressed in a man's denim trousers and shirt." The young woman's eyes sparkled brightly as she talked.

"See, what did I tell you?" Kate said, her hair catching the light as she nodded vigorously. "It's my prediction that you are going to find out that you missed being out here much more than you ever thought."

"No, I don't think so," Rachel responded, playing distractedly with the tassel on her nightgown. She was quiet for a moment, and then she said softly, "I do miss all those things, that's true . . . in fact I miss them terribly. But I'm just convinced that there is nothing out here for me."

"You mean there is no man for you?"

"Yes."

"You know, Rachel, when my husband was killed, all I wanted to do was escape the place where we had lived together. I wanted to get away from all the memories because, even though the memories were sweet, they hurt more than you can ever know. So I went to Philadelphia to start a new life. I actually even believed I might find another man but I have decided that if I do, it certainly won't be a Philadelphia dandy." Giggling, she concluded, "I saw enough of those gentlemen to last me a lifetime.''

Rachel laughed. ''How about a Wyoming dandy?'' she asked, her eyes twinkling mischievously. ''Someone like Damon Parker, for example.''

''Rachel!'' Kate gasped.

''Now don't tell me you haven't noticed him,'' Rachel teased.

Blushing, Kate looked down at her hands for a moment. Then she looked up and smiled broadly. ''Well, what if I have? Perhaps I did notice a little, but I think you're wrong calling him a dandy.'' A frown suddenly creased her forehead. ''You know, though, there is something about him.''

''Something good, or something bad?''

''Something that troubles me.''

''What is that?''

''Well, I couldn't exactly say,'' Kate continued. ''But during all those years my husband and I ran the hotel up in Antelope Springs, I saw more than my share of professional gamblers. I got to the point that I could pick one out the moment he came through the front door, no matter how he was dressed. Now, I'm sure Mr. Parker is indeed a professional gambler, just as he says. But I am also sure that there is more to that man than meets the eye.'' She paused, then added,

"And I have to admit that he is quite handsome."

Rachel countered. "Yes, well, I suppose some people may find him handsome. Not as handsome as Mr. Matthews, of course, but he is handsome."

"*Mr. Matthews*?" Kate blurted, before she realized that Rachel was teasing. She began laughing so hard that tears came. Finally she managed to get control of herself long enough to wipe her eyes and titter, "Oh, yes, Mr. Matthews is very handsome, but unfortunately for us, he's married."

Rachel put the back of her hand on her forehead imitating a stage tragedian. "Oh, how foul is fate, to find you one true love, only to have it denied because he belongs to another."

Both women laughed again, then hugged each other affectionately.

"Good night, Rachel," Kate said.

"Good night," Rachel replied. Rachel looked toward the bed where Lucy now lay sleeping. "I do hope the purgative helps Lucy. A long journey by stage is uncomfortable enough, without adding illness to the equation."

"Oh, I just know that she'll feel better tomorrow," Kate said.

Chapter Ten

It was dark, though the brightly shining moon provided a surprising amount of illumination. Deekus Tombs was sitting on a rock eating cold beans from a can. His right eye shined brightly in the moonlight, while his left was shielded from the moon by the drooping lid, the result of an old wound suffered in a jailhouse fight. The other prisoner had cut the muscles over Deekus's eyelid, leaving him permanently disfigured. Deekus had cut the other man's jugular vein, leaving him permanently dead.

Hawk Peters climbed up onto the ledge and looked toward the east.

"You seen anythin'?" Hawk asked.

"There ain't nothin' to see," Deekus replied. "It'll be another full day before the stage comes through here."

"Damn, couldn't we a found a better place to wait for it? I hate thinkin' about staying around here all day."

"You got anything better to do?" Deekus asked.

"I reckon not," Hawk admitted. He began relieving himself.

"Goddammit, Hawk, ain't you got no more manners than to piss that close to where a man is eatin'?" Deekus growled.

"Sorry, Deekus, I guess I just wasn't thinkin'," Hawk replied.

"That don't surprise me none. You don't never think."

"So, what time you reckon the stage'll be comin' by here?" Hawk asked.

"At four minutes past nine o'clock, Wednesday morning," Deekus replied sarcastically. "How the hell do I know?" he growled. "I'm not a time schedule board."

"I was just askin', is all," Hawk said.

"Don't ask. We'll see it when we see it."

"Where will that be, exactly?" Hawk asked.

Deekus pointed. "We'll see it first way down there, where the road takes a bend around the side of the mountain. After we see 'em, it'll take 'em half an hour to pull the grade, then they'll have to stop to give the horses a blow before startin' back down the other side. That's when we'll hit 'em."

Hawk laughed. "It's goin' to be like takin' candy from a baby."

Deekus finished the rest of his beans, then

stood up and threw the can away. It made a tiny, clinking noise when it hit the rocks far below.

"Ain't nothin' ever as easy as it seems," Deekus said, wiping his mouth with his shirtsleeve. "You 'n Silver 'n Prescott better be on your toes."

"We will be, Deekus, we will be," Hawk promised.

The night creatures called to each other as Quince stood looking toward Millersburg. A cloud passed over the moon then moved away. The little town that rose up like a ghost before him was bathed in silver moonlight. A couple of dozen buildings, half of which were lit up, fronted the main street. The biggest and most brightly lit building was the saloon at the far end of town.

Inside the saloon someone was playing a guitar and Quince could hear the music all the way out on the edge of town. The player was good, and the music spilled out in a steady beat with two or three poignant minor chords at the end of each phrase. An overall, single-string melody worked its way in and out of the chords like a thread of gold woven through the finest cloth. Quince liked that kind of music. It was mournful and lonesome, the kind of melody a man could let run through his mind during the long, quiet times.

He thought about going into town. No doubt by now word of his escape from prison had reached all the towns in Wyoming. But he couldn't recall ever having been in Millersburg, so he was reasonably sure that no one in town would recognize him. And even if word of his escape had reached this far, there were probably no reward posters out on him yet.

He saw a stagecoach sitting in front of the livery stable. The coach was dark and there was no team attached, but he knew it was the coach for Antelope Springs. Quince finally decided to go into town. He had never been in Millersburg before, so if he played it smart and confident, he was pretty sure that he could buy a ticket and get on the stage without anyone recognizing him. It would also be a pretty good place to hide, for no one would be expecting a wanted man to be using public transportation.

As Quince walked into town, he caught the smell of beans and spiced beef from one of the houses, and realized that it had been a couple of days since he had eaten well. His stomach growled in protest, and he decided that he would spend some of the money he had taken from the cowboy on food.

A dog let out a ribbony yap that was silenced by a kick or a thrown rock.

A baby cried, a sudden gargle that cracked the air like a bullwhip.

A housewife raised her voice in one of the houses, launching into some private tirade about something, sharing her anger with all who were within earshot.

Quince moved through the shadows until he reached the saloon. He was just about to step up onto the porch when two men came through the front door. In the lantern light that spilled out from the bright interior, Quince recognized one of the men as the sheriff of Antelope Springs.

Quickly, Quince jumped back into the shadows. *Will Jordan! What's he doing here in Millersburg?*

Quince stayed back in the shadows until Sheriff Jordan and the man who was with him had moved on down the street. Not until he was sure they were gone did he go inside.

Moving as unobtrusively as he could, Quince stepped up to the bar, waiting quietly until the bartender saw him. When the bartender noticed him, he was slightly startled.

"Damn, mister, I didn't see you come in," he said. "You been standin' there long?"

"Not too long," Quince answered easily.

"What can I get you?"

"A beer," Quince said. "And some food. What've you got?"

"Boiled ham and fried potatoes," the bartender replied.

"That'll be fine," Quince said. He paid for the

beer, then nodded toward a nearby table. "I'll be right over there."

Felton couldn't believe his luck when he saw Quince Fremont come into the saloon. Felton was standing at the opposite end of the bar, blocked from Quince's direct view by the cast-iron stove.

Felton watched as Quince said a few words to the bartender, then took his beer toward a nearby table. Felton slowly pulled his gun from his holster, then, holding it down by his side so it wouldn't be obvious, he stepped away from the bar.

Quince was just pulling the chair out from the table when out of the corner of his eye, he saw someone moving toward him with his pistol in his hand. Though he didn't know his assailant's name, he recognized him as one of Deekus Tombs's gang.

Quince wondered, briefly, if the whole gang was here and if he might be surrounded. But there was no time to dwell on that, because the man coming toward him was already bringing his pistol to bear. Quince slipped his own pistol out of his holster and suddenly the room was shattered with the roar of two pistols exploding.

The other patrons in the saloon yelled out and scrambled for cover. White smoke billowed out from both guns, filling the center of the room.

As the cloud began to roll away, Felton stared

through the drifting white smoke, glaring at Quince. "You killed my brother," he said. "And now I've . . .". that was as far as he got. Coherent words were replaced by a gagging rattle way back in his throat. His eyes glazed over and he pitched forward, his gun clattering to the floor.

That threat over, Quince looked around the saloon, checking to see if any of Deekus's other men were lying in wait for him. His pistol was cocked and he was ready to fire a second time.

He looked back at the man he had just killed, then holstered his pistol. Seeing him put his pistol back in the holster, the other patrons began to slowly reappear from under tables, behind the bar and stove, and even from under the staircase.

A lawman came running in then, but seeing that it was all over, he put his gun away. He looked toward the body on the floor.

Every fiber in Quince's body told him to bolt and run but he knew he wouldn't get very far. His only hope was to bluff it out.

"Who did it?" the lawman asked.

"He did," the bartender said, nodding toward Quince. "But it was a fair fight. The fella on the floor drew first."

"That's right, Deputy," one of the others said. "This fella had his gun drawn before the fight even commenced."

After that, several men at once began telling

the story, each adding embellishments from his own perspective. When they were finished the lawman came over to Quince.

"Mister, you want to tell us what this was all about?"

"His name is Pogue. He's one of Deekus Tombs's men," Quince explained. Although he wasn't that familiar with Pogue on sight, he knew this man had to be one of them because, in his dying declaration, he had accused Quince of killing his brother. The only brothers riding for Deekus were the Pogue brothers.

"Which Pogue is it?"

"I don't know," Quince replied. "It doesn't much matter."

"That there's Felton Pogue," a bar girl said. She was standing at the foot of the stairs, and though she was fully dressed, her disheveled appearance suggested that she had just dressed, and had done so quickly. "At least that's what he told me his name was."

"Felton Pogue," the deputy said. He nodded. "Yes, I believe I do recognize that name from some paper we've got on him down at the sheriff's office." He looked at Quince. "What did you mean when you said, it doesn't matter?"

"Because they're both dead now. I killed the other one a few days ago."

"You a lawman?"

Quince shook his head. "No."

"A bounty hunter?"

"No, I'm not that, either," he said. "I just happened to be at the wrong place at the wrong time."

"What's your name, mister?"

"My name's . . . Cornwallis," Quince said. "Lester Cornwallis." He had no idea where the name came from, but he knew he couldn't use his own name.

"Well, Mr. Cornwallis, soon as we get word from the capital, I reckon you'll be due a reward. You staying in town for the night?"

"Yes, sure, if there's a reward," Quince replied, feigning enthusiasm over the prospect.

"Good. You stop by the sheriff's office tomorrow sometime. By then he ought to have ever'-thing taken care of, and he'll give you a draft you can take to the bank."

"I'll be there," Quince said.

"You two men, drag him out of here," the bartender ordered. "Then come on back. I reckon an occasion like this ought to be good for a round of drinks on the house."

With a shout of pleasure, everyone in the saloon rushed to the bar to put in their order. Quince forced himself to stay at the table until after he finished his meal, then with a cheery wave at the others, he stepped out into the darkness. There was no doubt in his mind that when the sheriff started getting information on the man he had just shot, he would also get information on him.

Though Quince would have liked the reward money, and dearly needed it, he had no intention of staying around that long. Slipping into the shadows, he darted around to the back of the saloon, then left town. He would catch up with the stagecoach tomorrow, somewhere out on the road, north of town.

Chapter Eleven

It was barely light when the coach pulled out of Millersburg, and all the passengers had reclaimed the same seats they had occupied the day before. By now they had learned the skill of getting comfortable in a close and rough-riding coach, and they leaned their heads back, propped their feet against the seats opposite to minimize the jostling, then quickly dropped off to sleep.

Damon Parker dreamed again, and again his sleep was troubled by disquieting visions from his past.

"Are you sure you want to go through with this?" the doctor asked. "The malignancy has progressed much too far . . . and as you well know, such a procedure has never been tried before."

"Not in America, but it has been successfully demonstrated by Andral in Paris," Damon replied, looking down toward the operating table. He then lowered the sheet that had been covering the face of the anesthetized patient . . . it was the same beautiful young woman to whom he had give his guarantee that she would be all right.

The assisting surgeon shook his head. "Dr. Parker, I have the utmost respect for your surgical skills, as you well know, but removing a malignant tumor? At best it is extremely difficult, and it is further complicated here because you are removing it from her abdomen. She may die on the operating table."

"If the tumor isn't removed she will die, and that is for certain. Besides, I gave her my word that she will come through this successfully."

Shaking his head again, the assisting surgeon declared, "I only pray that you won't live to regret a promise made in desperation."

Damon ignored the comment and picked up his scalpel to begin the delicate operation. All went well until he was about to close the abdomen, then suddenly the woman began to hemorrhage. Although the young doctor worked frantically to stop the bleeding, the woman's blood pressure dropped precipitously, and despite Damon's best efforts, she died on the table.

Barely hearing the other surgeon telling him that it was not his fault, that she would have died anyway, even had he not performed the risky operation, Damon looked down at her life-less body. He then stared at his hands, covered with her blood. The hands that had been so successful in dozens and dozens of operations had failed him now, when he needed them most.

Holding his hands up in front of him, he cried out in agony. "My God, what have I done? If I had not been so eager to try the new procedure, if I had not been so arrogant as to think I could do what dozens of other surgeons could not, she would still be alive. Then it would have been up to God, not me, whether she lived or died."

"You mustn't do this to yourself, Dr. Kensington," his colleague insisted. "You let yourself get too close to the patient."

"I was going to marry her, Doctor," Damon retorted coldly. "She was my fiancée. How much closer could I get?"

He looked down at the table and then picked up the lifeless hand of the young woman. "I'm sorry, Deborah," he whispered in a choked voice, kissing the hand tenderly before releasing it.

Turning his back on the operating table, he dropped his scalpel on the floor and walked away, determined never to pick up a surgical instrument again. He hurried out of the operating theater and closed the door firmly behind him.

*　　*　　*

Damon awakened with a start, and it took a few moments for him to realize that he was riding the stagecoach to Antelope Springs, not walking the halls of Boston Mercy Hospital.

Dr. D. Parker Kensington had left the hospital and removed all his funds from the bank. He went to the railroad depot that very day, altering his name and taking the first train going west. Within weeks he had become a professional gambler, using his skilled hands to manipulate decks of cards rather than surgical tools, and plying the saloons and gaming houses all over the West.

For the five years he had been out West, he had not communicated with anyone from his past. He had not sent so much as one word to any of his friends or colleagues back in Boston telling them where he was or what he was doing.

Once, about a year ago, he was surprised to read an article about himself in a newspaper in Denver.

WHEREABOUTS OF NOTED SURGEON STILL UNKNOWN, the headline had read. The story related how, after losing his betrothed on the operating table years earlier, D. Parker Kensington, M.D., had disappeared. According to the article, some people believed he had gone to Europe to practice medicine, while others believed they had spotted him on Boston's skid row. One person swore he had become a ship's surgeon, sailing the big windjammer to China. No one had guessed where he really was, or what he was doing.

The others in the coach all stirred awake as well, and as the gambler looked out at the eastern sky, he estimated that the sun had been up for nearly an hour. He felt the coach begin to slow and as he glanced ahead, he saw a man standing in the road, waving his arms to flag them down.

On top of the coach, Beans raised his shotgun, but Gib put out his hand to stop him. "Hold it," he said. "I know that man. Fact is, he's ridden shotgun himself from time to time." Gib hauled back on the reins and set the brake on the coach, bringing it to a halt.

Down on the road, Quince smiled broadly in recognition. "Hello, Gib," the escaped convict called up to him. "It's good to see you."

"I wish I could say the same for you," Gib replied.

Quince frowned. "You mean you aren't happy to see me?"

"Any other time, maybe. Not now," Gib said. He nodded toward the coach as, behind him, the door opened and Will Jordan stepped out.

Jordan was holding a gun, leveled at Quince. "Hi, kid," he said.

"Sheriff," Quince replied.

"Wish you hadn't chosen my road to be walkin' on. I heard about you breakin' out of the penitentiary."

"Damn," Quince said, half jokingly. "I was hoping I could convince you I got a pardon."

"I guess you know I'm goin' to have to take you prisoner."

Quince sighed, then smiled. "Well, I reckon it's better than dying out here in the cold," he said.

"Give me your gun, kid," Jordan said.

Quince thought about it for a moment. The way the sheriff was holding his pistol, Quince could have drawn down on him. But if he drew, he would have to shoot, and he had no wish to do that. He sighed, then smiled. "All right," he said, taking his pistol from his holster, then holding it out, butt first.

Jordan stepped in front of his young prisoner then put handcuffs on his wrists.

"Do you have to do that, Will?"

" 'Fraid so."

"What if I give you my word I wouldn't try to escape?"

"Oh, you could give me your word, kid, and I'm sure you would mean it," Jordan said. "But first chance you got, you'd skedaddle. Hell, I would, too. Wouldn't be much of a man if you didn't."

"I guess you got me pegged," Quince said.

Ethan Matthews had been leaning out the window watching what was going on. When he saw Jordan put handcuffs on Quince, he leapt down from the coach, clutching the black satchel tightly to his chest. "Now wait a minute. Just you hold on here, Sheriff," Matthews blustered. "You don't really intend to bring that outlaw along with us, do you? I mean, especially in view of what we're carrying on this stage."

Quince squinted at Matthews, then nodded toward the little black bag. "Is that where the hundred thousand dollars is?" he asked.

Will Jordan's mouth fell wide open. "What the hell?" he blurted. "Is there anyone on God's green earth who *doesn't* know what we're carrying on this stage?"

"You've got me," Quince replied.

"I'd be interested in hearing how you found out," Jordan said.

"I happened across Deekus Tombs," Quince replied.

"You were running with him?"

"Not with him, after him," Quince said. "I plan to use him to prove I'm innocent."

"Even if you caught him, you wouldn't be able to change anything."

"Oh, yes I could, if I forced him to tell the truth."

"Forced testimony is discounted testimony.

Anyway, what does that have to do with the hundred thousand dollars?"

"Like I said, I stumbled across his camp the other night, and while I was sneaking around, I overheard a conversation. Deekus told his men they'd soon have a hundred thousand dollars to divvy up. That's when I happened to kick loose a piece of shale and they got on to me. I exchanged gunfire with them, and killed one of the Pogue brothers."

"Wait a minute, that was you last night? In the saloon back in town?" Jordan asked.

"You heard about it?"

The sheriff nodded. "Yes, they were talking about it this morning. They said it was a man named . . ."

"Cornwallis?" Quince finished for him with a laugh.

"Yeah, that's it."

"Sheriff, you didn't think I was going to give them my real name, did you?"

"No, I don't guess that would be all that smart," Jordan said. He stroked his jaw. "But you've sure left me with a bit of a problem."

"He ain't the problem, Sheriff," Gib said. "The problem is Deekus Tombs. He knows we're carrying the money."

"That's right," Jordan said.

"Well, it makes no difference how he knows,"

Quince said. "The point is, he does know and that means he'll be lying in wait somewhere ahead." Quince smiled. "So I'll be getting another chance at him after all."

"Sheriff, I refuse to be a passenger or to allow money I am carrying to be on the same stage with an escaped convict," Matthews grumbled.

"Well, I'm not leaving this man out here, Mr. Matthews," Jordan replied, his increasing impatience with Matthews obvious in his voice. "For one thing, it wouldn't be Christian. And for another, he's a wanted man and I'm a sheriff. I have to do my duty. So you've got no choice, unless you want to get out here and walk back to Millersburg to wait for the next stage."

"It's a disgrace, an absolute disgrace," the bank clerk muttered. "If anything happens, I shall hold you personally responsible. That's a promise."

Quince was about to climb up to the top of the coach when Jordan motioned him toward the passenger compartment. "No," he said. "You'll ride inside where I can keep an eye on you. There's no room on the seats, but you can ride on the floor."

Shrugging, Quince remarked, "Well, I'm not going to enjoy it as much, but I'll oblige you." So saying, he stepped inside, giving everyone a casual, sweeping glance. "Hello, folks. Hope you don't mind the intrus—" He stopped at the sight of Rachel Kincaid. "Rachel," he gasped. "What . . . what are you doing here? I didn't think I'd ever see you again. I heard you had gone back East."

"Hello, Mr. Fremont," Rachel replied coolly.

"*Mister* Fremont?" Quince retorted. "When did it become Mr. Fremont? It never was before."

Rachel frowned at the handcuffs on Quince's wrists. "You were never a bank robber before," she countered.

"I'm not a bank robber now," he insisted.

"The court says you are."

"I was set-up."

"You expect people to actually believe that?"

"I don't know," Quince admitted. "But I guess I hoped you, of all people, would believe it."

On top of the coach, the driver whistled and shouted to his team. With a resounding crack of the whip, the stagecoach got underway again.

"Answer me, Rachel," Quince almost shouted above the clacking wheels. "Did you really believe that my brother and I robbed that bank?"

Rachel turned and faced him. "No," she answered quietly.

"We were set-up by Deekus Tombs," Quince said.

"I was back East during your trial, but my father sent me the newspaper. I know you testified that you were set-up."

"It was the truth, every word of it."

"Then why didn't the jury believe you?" Rachel asked.

"Perhaps I can answer that question," Will Jordan suggested. "If you read the newspapers your father sent you, you know that I testified on Quince's behalf."

"Yes, I read that."

Smiling at the lawman, Quince said, "I've never forgotten how you gave testimony on my behalf. I'll be forever grateful to you."

"I just wish I could've done more. But to answer your question, Miss Kincaid, the reason the jury didn't believe him was because he wasn't on trial."

"He wasn't on trial?"

"No, ma'am. It was the community of Theresa that was on trial."

"What do you mean by that, Sheriff?" Rachel asked.

"Well, when Deekus Tombs and his boys held up that town, the whole town turned out to defend it," Jordan explained. "But you may recall that Tombs got away and several people got killed. That made them even more determined to run Tombs down and get revenge. So when they found Quince and Cole, they figured they had redeemed themselves somewhat. Now, don't forget that the jury was made up of citizens from that same town, some of the same folks who had been shooting at Tombs earlier. They weren't about to deny the community its success in bringing someone they thought was in his gang to justice. I don't think they really intended to sentence an innocent man, I think they just refused to accept defeat . . . and if Quince had been proven innocent in their eyes, it would have been a defeat."

Kate looked down at Quince.

"My husband was killed in that bank holdup," she said. "And I must confess that, at first, I had only the harshest of feelings for you. But the more I thought about it, the more convinced I was that you didn't do it. After all, I'd known you and your brother for a long time. And the Cole and Quince Fremont I knew couldn't possibly have done such a thing."

"Mrs. O'Leary, you don't know how glad I am to hear you say that," Quince said. "I thought the world of Mr. O'Leary. I was saddened to hear of his death and even sadder to think that anyone would believe I had something to do with it."

"This is a lot of poppycock!" Ethan Matthews fumed. "Sheriff, would you listen to yourself and the others? You're saying the only reason Fremont was found guilty was because he was tried in Theresa. But if the people in this coach are any indication, he would have been found innocent had he been tried in Antelope Springs! So nothing has been proven. The real test would be to try him somewhere other than Theresa or Antelope Springs."

"That's just what I hoped to do by breaking out of prison," Quince remarked wryly. "I wanted to capture Deekus Tombs, then force another trial in a neutral location. I would be quite willing to accept the decision of that jury."

"If, as you say, you have already killed the Pogue brothers, then it would appear to me that you have no intention of capturing Tombs, but plan to murder him and the rest of his gang instead."

"I did kill the Pogue brothers, but I didn't murder them," Quince said. "It was self-defense."

"Nearly every killer makes that claim," Matthews said.

"The man who shot Pogue in the saloon last night was acting in self-defense," Damon said. "Or at least, so said the witnesses I spoke to this morning."

"Well, I'm not from Theresa or Antelope Springs, Mr. Fremont, and were I to serve on a jury hearing your case, I would find you guilty," the little bank clerk declared.

"Without hearing the evidence?" Quince asked.

"Seeing you here in handcuffs is evidence enough for me," Matthews said. "You are an escaped criminal, and I intend to regard you as such." Facing the lawman, Matthews added, "And what's more, Sheriff Jordan, I demand that you do so as well. After all, you are a public servant, and I am carrying a great deal of money that is desperately needed by the people in your own county. How do you think it would look to the ranchers there if the money they needed was lost because of your incompetence?"

Clearly trying to control his temper, the sheriff muttered, "Mr. Matthews, why don't you just relax and keep quiet. I'll see to it that the money gets through all right."

Sitting on the floor of the coach with his back against the door and his knees drawn up before him, Quince looked up at Damon and smiled. "I don't believe I've had the pleasure," he announced.

The gambler smiled down at him. "Damon. Damon Parker."

"I'm—"

"Quince Fremont, I know." Damon smiled. "Your reputation precedes you, Mr. Fremont."

"Call me Quince."

"Quince . . ." Lucy piped up, but her mother quickly shushed her.

"Lucy, you are not to call an adult by his first name. You are to call him Mr. Fremont."

"But, Mama, he just said to call him Quince."

"He told Mr. Parker to call him Quince. Mr. Parker is an adult, you are a child."

Laughing, the prisoner declared, "I don't mind if she calls me Quince. Friends call each other by their first name, and after all, I'd like for Lucy to be my friend. If it's all right with you, Mrs. O'Leary."

"Is it all right, Mama?"

Sighing, Kate conceded. "I suppose."

"How are you doing, Lucy?" Quince asked.

"I'm not feeling real good," Lucy said. "Have you ever been sick?"

Quince looked from the girl to her mother, then back again. "Well, I sure have, and I'm sorry to hear that you are feeling so poorly. But I'm sure you'll be better real soon."

After that, they rode in silence for a while, the passengers lost in their own thoughts. Several times Quince glanced up at Rachel, sensing that she had been watching him from the corner of her eye. But each time he looked up, she glanced away, refusing to acknowledge him. Finally, Quince gave up and, pulling his hat down over his eyes, allowed himself to take a nap.

Kate watched the interplay between the two

and smiled inwardly. It was obvious to anyone that they were attracted to each other. Why wasn't it obvious to them? She thought to herself. Perhaps it was, but they were just fighting it off for reasons of their own.

She looked down at Lucy, then brushed the hair back from her daughter's face.

"How is she doing?" Will asked.

"She's being very good," Kate said. "But I really don't think that doctor did the least bit of good for her last night." She shook her head. "I might have more confidence if he had been sober."

"Mrs. O'Leary, her face appears flushed," Damon said. "Does she have a fever?"

Kate felt Lucy's face, then nodded. "Yes, she does." Taking the canteen from the floor, she wet her handkerchief and placed it on Lucy's forehead. The little girl looked up at her mother through pain-wracked eyes.

Removing his own handkerchief from his pocket, Damon handed it to her. "Wet this one as well, and put it on the back of her neck," he suggested. "It will help bring the fever down."

"Thank you," Kate replied, smiling at the gambler. She reached into her reticule. "I should probably give her another dose of this purgative, though it doesn't seem to be doing any good."

"May I see it?" Damon asked.

"Yes, of course," Kate replied. She handed the little green bottle to him.

Damon removed the stopper from the bottle, smelled it, made a face, and shook his head.

"Mrs. O'Leary, I would advise you against giving Lucy any more of this."

Matthews looked over at Damon and snorted in distaste. "I hardly see where a man like you, a gambler, comes off telling someone not to administer a curative that was prescribed by a medical doctor," he remarked.

"A drunken doctor," Kate pointed out in a sharp voice.

"But a doctor nevertheless, madam. Whereas this man is nothing but a common gambler."

"That doesn't mean he can't have a gift for doctoring," Will Jordan put in. "I've known lots of people with such a gift, and if they've got common sense and sober thought to go along with it, I'd say they're worth listening to as much as anybody."

Lucy suddenly pleaded. "Mama, I don't want to take any more of that. It tastes horrible!" She had no sooner spoken the words than she leapt off her mother's lap, pushed her way to the window, then stuck her head outside. She gagged a few times, though nothing came up from her empty stomach. Her face was even paler when she climbed back onto her mother's lap.

Shaking her head, Kate O'Leary declared,

"We'll listen to Mr. Parker. You don't have to take any more."

"Thank you, Mama," Lucy said. She looked at Damon and smiled wanly. "And thank you, Mr. Parker, for telling Mama I shouldn't take it."

"You're welcome," Damon said. "I just want you to get to feeling better."

Chapter Twelve

The stagecoach passengers had become accustomed to the long, tiring, bone-jarring ride, and throughout the rest of the day one or more of them could frequently be found dozing. Damon Parker managed to relieve some of the monotony of the waking hours of the journey by demonstrating card tricks for the others, and everyone was impressed by the dexterity of his hands and fingers. Everyone, that is, but Ethan Matthews. He made an obvious show of his total disdain for anything so trivial as card tricks, and he pointedly ignored the display, staring glumly out the window.

After the card tricks, the passengers began exchanging stories. Will Jordan had been a trooper in Custer's cavalry. He was with Reno during Custer's last fight and he told of the bloody massacre at Little Bighorn.

Kate listened attentively and then added a little bit of information that the sheriff had omitted. "He's much too modest a man to tell this part of it," she explained, "and I wouldn't have known myself had a visiting army officer not informed my husband and me one day. You see, Sheriff Jordan was awarded the Medal of Honor for his part in that battle."

"The Medal of Honor!" Damon exclaimed. "Well, Sheriff, I am very impressed."

"All I did was get a little water for some of my comrades," Will mumbled. "It hardly seemed like something to get the medal for. Still," he added, a faraway look on his face, "it was a proud moment when President Grant pinned it on me."

When it was Kate's turn to entertain the others, she told a story of the night Jenny Lind, the Swedish Nightingale, had stayed at the hotel she and her husband ran. "She was such a lovely person, and had the most beautiful singing voice."

"Yes," Jordan said. "I remember when she was in town. She gave a performance at the Golden Peacock Theater. So many people came that there was barely enough room to stand during one of her shows."

Rachel then related some of her experiences in Boston. She talked about the wonders she had seen there, such things as the telephone, elevators, magic lantern shows, and Mr. Edison's talking machine.

"I was reminded of all the mean tricks I've seen our cowboys pull on the dudes from the East," she said, giggling, "for I was a 'rube' from out West and as fair game for their jokes as any tenderfoot ever was for a bit of Western fun. Once, when we were painting one of the rooms of the dormitory, the other girls sent me to a store to buy some spotted paint."

The others in the coach laughed.

"I know, I know," Rachel agreed, "it sounds perfectly ridiculous to think I would fall for something like that. But you must remember, my mind had been bedazzled with all the inventions of modern society . . . inventions we had never even heard of out here, much less seen. I was perfectly willing to believe that there was such a thing as spotted paint."

Quince was next in the line of storytellers, and he soon was regaling everyone with the hilarious story of a joke his brother had once played on him. As she listened to it, Rachel thought perhaps his story told something about the man. No one else knew the real events, and he could have easily turned it around so that his brother, and not he, had been the butt of the joke, but he did not. Instead, he accepted the embarrassment of the moment without hesitation.

When everyone had fallen silent, Kate looked over at the gambler. "What about you, Mr. Parker? Surely with all your adventures, you have a story you could share with us?"

Damon looked thoughtful for a moment, then he told about a balloon ascension he had once made in France. "I went aloft in a balloon with the celebrated aeronaut Gaston Tissandier," he told the others. "It was a most exciting excursion, and I was given the job of monitoring the other passengers for oxygen deprivation, while of course making certain that I didn't get into trouble myself."

"Oh, my, that sounds very exciting," Kate said, her eyes flashing as she stared intently at him. "What happened?"

"As we got to fourteen thousand feet, we all began to get a little giddy," Damon said. "From there on up, I insisted that we use the oxygen in greater and greater doses. Then, disaster struck. The gas-relief valve froze on the balloon, and for a while we were afraid we would keep going up and up without stop."

"What if you had gone all the way to the moon?" Lucy asked.

"Oh, honey, that isn't possible," Damon explained. "The balloon can go only as high as there is air, and the air stops."

"It stops?" Jordan asked. "What do you mean it stops?"

"Air surrounds the earth . . . like a great sea.

And just as a fish can come to the top of the sea but can't rise above that, so too can we go to the top of the air in a balloon. But we can't go beyond that."

"What is above the air?" Quince asked.

"Just empty space. In fact, that is exactly what some scientists call it."

"What happened when you got to the top of all the air?" Kate asked.

"Well, we didn't make it all the way to the top. Fortunately, the balloon burst, and our descent was assured . . . although at a far more rapid rate than we would have wished," he concluded wryly.

"How was it that you weren't killed?" Kate asked, now on the edge of her seat from the excitement and tension of the story.

"When the gas bag exploded, it formed a huge inverted cup, much like an umbrella," Damon explained. "Consequently, it set us down as gently as a feather."

"My, what a marvelous adventure!" Kate declared, her eyes shining with pleasure, and the others added their own words of appreciation for his story.

"Poppycock!" Matthews scoffed. "You might have the others convinced, Parker, but not me. What would a gambler be doing in France?"

"I haven't always been a gambler, Mr. Matthews," Damon murmured. "You, on the other hand, have probably always been a jackass."

Damon's rejoinder brought an outburst of laughter from the others in the coach. Matthews merely clutched his black satchel even more tightly while he fumed in silence.

Shortly after that the coach stopped, and Will Jordan leaned out of the window, a slight breeze ruffling his gray hair. "I wonder why we're stopping here," he said as he pulled his head back inside.

"We're near a way station, I believe," Quince said.

"Sheriff!" Gib called down from up on the driver's seat. "Sheriff, you want to step out of the coach for a minute?"

"Sure thing," Jordan replied, opening the door and climbing down. He walked a few steps forward and then looked up at Gib who was standing on his seat and pointing toward a small cluster of buildings about a quarter of a mile ahead.

"That's the Belle Fourche Station," Gib said. "We're supposed to change teams and spend the night there . . . but I don't know. I don't like the looks of it. I don't see no smoke nor nothin'. It just don't appear to be right."

Shading his eyes, the lawman looked ahead. Finally, shaking his head, he suggested, "Well, we aren't going to find out anything by staying here, so you may as well drive on in. But keep your eyes open real good."

"Hey, Sheriff," Beans called, his weathered face screwed up with concern, "are you any good with a long gun?"

"I reckon I can hit what I'm aiming at," Jordan answered laconically. "Why do you ask?"

"Well, sir, aside from this here shotgun, I got me two Winchesters up here in the boot. I'd be obliged if'n you'd take one of 'em and come up on top till we get into the station."

Nodding in agreement, Gib added, "Yeah, as a matter of fact, I believe I'd appreciate that myself, if you don't mind."

"All right," Jordan answered.

"Sheriff, what's wrong?" Ethan Matthews called, sticking his head out the window. "What's going on?"

"Mr. Matthews, you and the others just stay put inside," Jordan ordered. "I'm going to ride on top of the coach until we get into the station."

"What about this escaped criminal we have in here?" Matthews asked in a disbelieving, reproving voice. "Are you just going to leave him in the coach with us? We are unarmed and helpless. If he decides to try something, who will protect us from him?"

"Don't be afraid of him, Matthews. You've got

the ladies to watch out for you," Jordan countered.

The others laughed at the remark, which only served to rile the banker more. "See here, Sheriff! This is no laughing matter," Matthews said angrily. "I demand you do something about this prisoner."

"Mr. Matthews, you certainly are one for making demands," Jordan growled. Sighing, he said, "All right, Quince, why don't you climb up on top with me?"

"Suits me," Quince agreed easily. Exiting the coach, he climbed up to the luggage rack and then sat down and leaned back against the trunks. Jordan climbed up alongside him then took one of the rifles from Beans.

"All right, Gib," Jordan said, nodding, "you drive her on in and let's see what we can find out."

Nodding, the driver nudged Beans. "Beans, you keep your eyes skinned. If you see anythin', you let me know and I'll snap a whip over these critters so fast, they'll think they're gettin' ready to run that there derby they run down in Kentucky."

"I'll do it," Beans said.

Gib started the team forward, and the coach rolled slowly for the remaining quarter of a mile. A few minutes later it pulled into the depot. Halfway between the corral and the main building, they saw a man lying on his stomach. He wasn't moving.

"That there is Angus Clark," Gib announced softly, pointing to the body as he halted the team. "He's one of the hostlers here."

Just then the door opened on the coach and Jordan ordered sharply, "Stay in the coach, all of you! We may have to leave fast."

Damon called back, "Sheriff, I'd like to take a closer look at that man over there, if you don't mind. Perhaps he's still alive."

Weighing the idea for a moment, the lawman relented. "All right, I reckon you can take a look if you want to. I'm pretty damn sure there's nothing you're gonna be able to do for him, though."

Stepping out of the coach, Damon walked over to the body. Squatting down behind him, he put his hand on the man's cheeks to test his body temperature. He then moved the hostler's arms and legs to test the degree of rigor mortis.

Turning to the driver, Jordan asked Gib, "See anything?"

Both the driver and shotgun guard were standing on top of the stage, sweeping the area carefully with their gazes.

"No, I don't see nothin'," Gib replied. "How 'bout you, Beans?"

"No, I don't see nothin', either. Maybe I'll just climb down and take a look around," he volunteered and then flicked a glance at the lawman. "If that's all right with you, Sheriff."

"Yeah, sure. Go ahead," Jordan replied, never taking his eyes from the scene.

Beans hopped down from the coach and began looking around the station. It was so quiet that the silence itself became a presence. That was particularly evident when the windmill behind the one-story log building responded to a breeze and suddenly swung around with a loud squeaking clank and then started spinning.

Like the others, Jordan was startled by the sudden sound, and he swung his rifle toward the stable, only to see the windmill whirling into life.

Quince Fremont stepped down from the coach and looked up at Jordan. "Sheriff, have you noticed that there are no horses in the stable?" he asked, motioning toward the corral.

"Yeah," Jordan answered. "I noticed that."

Beans was walking toward the main building. He neared the front porch then stopped. He stared for a moment and then came back to the coach, walking back at a much quicker pace.

"What is it?" Gib asked. "What did you find?"

"There's two more bodies over there," he said, pointing. "I think one of 'em might be the stationmaster. Both of 'em's been shot."

Jordan rubbed his chin thoughtfully, then

asked, "What do you think, Beans? Is this the work of Indians?"

"No, I don't think so," Beans answered, scratching his sparsely covered head. "Leastwise, whoever done this sure ain't acted like no Indians I've ever saw. All of 'em was shot, and there's no scalpin' and no knife wounds."

"Well, whoever it was, I don't think they're around here anymore," Gib offered. "I mean, it seems too damn quiet for that."

Damon came back to the stage and looked up at Jordan. "If it means anything, that man over there hasn't been dead for more than three or four hours."

Nodding, Jordan responded. "Being a sheriff, I shouldn't say this, but since there are women and a child on the stage, I hope it means that whoever did it is three or four hours from here by now."

"Yeah, that's what I hope, too," Beans said.

"Sheriff, if you don't mind, I'm going to let my passengers out," Gib said.

"Wait for another moment or two," Jordan said.

"Come on, Will, I hope you ain't planning on keepin' these folks in the coach forever," Gib said. "They got to be able to get out and stretch their legs a bit. Especially the ladies, if you know what I mean."

"I'm not going to make you hold them much

longer," Jordan said. "Just long enough to check in and around the outhouses, to make certain there are no unpleasant surprises waiting inside. In the meantime, Beans, you want to get a tarp or something over those bodies?"

"I'll do better'n that, Sheriff," Beans offered, starting back toward the barn. "There's gotta be some shovels around here somewhere. I'll get 'em buried."

Will Jordan watched Beans's retreating back for a moment, then he hopped down and made a thorough check of the area. Coming back to the stagecoach, he opened the door and spoke to the passengers.

"All right, folks, it seems safe enough. You can come on out now, if you want to."

"Thanks," Kate said, brushing back a strand of her hair. Her skin was covered with a light patina of sweat and she was fanning both herself and Lucy with a small, handheld fan. "I don't think I could have stayed in this coach for another minute."

As the passengers wandered around the station, Gib and Beans dug graves for the three dead men. "We'll leave a letter for the next coach that comes through here, tellin' 'em what we did," Gib explained to Jordan. "I don't want to take them poor fellas on the stage with us, but there's no way we can just leave them lyin' out here."

"I agree," Jordan said.

Coming alongside the men, Kate looked at Gib and asked, "Mr. Crabtree, would it be all right if I look around the kitchen? Perhaps I can find something to fix for our supper."

"I think that would be a grand idea," Gib said. "I hadn't thought of it but, now that you mention it, I am mighty hungry."

"How 'bout a little help in the kitchen?" Rachel asked.

"Thanks, that would be nice," Kate said. She put her arm around Lucy's shoulders. "Come along, child, you stay inside out of everyone's way."

"Those men are dead, aren't they, Mama?" Lucy said, quietly.

"Yes, dear."

"I don't like it when people die."

"No, dear, no one likes it," Kate said. "But dying is as much a part of God's plan as living is. Now come along. We've got to get something cooked, if we want to eat."

"I don't want to eat."

"Oh, honey, you barely touched your supper last night, you didn't eat a bite for breakfast this morning, we had that nice lunch that the hotel made for us to bring in the coach, and you didn't eat that, either. You have to eat something."

"I'm not hungry," Lucy insisted.

Kate leaned down and kissed her daughter on the forehead. "Oh, dear me," she said. "Whatever could be wrong with my little girl?"

As Kate, Lucy, and Rachel went into the building, Ethan Matthews watched from his seated position on the boarding step of the coach. An annoyed expression was on his face when Will Jordan neared. The bank clerk pointed toward Quince Fremont, who was wandering around the yard examining the tracks that had been left in the dirt.

"Sheriff," the little man asked, "are you just going to let your prisoner roam around free like that?"

"He's not exactly free, Mr. Matthews," Jordan answered. "As you can clearly see, his hands are manacled."

"That isn't enough," Matthews said. "He should be chained to a tree or to the wheel of the stage or something. He shouldn't be allowed to roam around like that. For all we know, he might have been the one who killed all these people here. You are putting every person on this coach in jeopardy."

Jordan shook his head and sighed audibly. He stared at Matthews as if he couldn't believe him. "What the hell is wrong with you, Matthews? You know damned well Quince didn't kill those men."

"How do I know that? He is a convicted criminal, isn't he?"

"Being convicted and actually being guilty is two different things," Jordan replied. "And even so, the court didn't find him guilty of murder. Besides, he was with us."

"He wasn't with us last night," Matthews insisted. "He joined us this morning, if you recall."

"He was afoot, and it has taken us all day by stage to get here."

"So . . . who is to say that he wasn't mounted? Perhaps his horse went lame along the way and that was why he was out on the trail looking for a ride. Or maybe he is riding with us just to establish his alibi."

"Now you aren't making any sense at all. You heard what Mr. Parker said. These men haven't been dead for more than three or four hours. That means Quince couldn't have done it."

"In other words, you're taking the word of a professional gambler on how long these unfortunate victims have been dead?" Matthews asked, scornfully.

"Why not? Mr. Parker seems to have an uncommon amount of sense about some things."

"Nevertheless, I am making a note of this," the clerk promised, "along with the several other errors in judgment you have made. I intend to hold you accountable for every one of them."

"You just go ahead and do that, you dried up little turd."

Gasping, Matthews stood up quickly and pointed at Jordan. "And that, too! Don't think for one moment your rude behavior hasn't been noted."

There was a moment of silence, then Quince called out to Jordan. "Will, you want to come over here and take a look at this?"

More than willing to oblige, Jordan left Matthews and walked over to where Quince was standing.

"That little weasel giving you trouble, is he?" Quince asked.

"He's trying to," Jordan admitted. "But I don't plan to pay any more attention to him. But never mind him—what have you found?"

Raising his manacled hands, Quince pointed to some hoofprint in the dirt. "You see this tie-bar shoe?" he asked. "While I was sneaking around Deekus's camp the other night, I noticed that one of the horses was shod this way." He gestured toward the main building, adding, "The reason this didn't look like Indians is 'cause it wasn't. It was some of Deekus Tombs's work."

"Deekus Tombs, huh?" Jordan mused. "I was afraid of that. And if they know about the money, that means they are after us. But what gets me is why did they have to kill everyone here?"

"I imagine they wanted to run the horses away so they could keep us from having a fresh team," Quince answered. "That would sure give them an advantage, and the only way they could do that would be to kill the men who work here." He shrugged, then added, "I suppose the only reason they didn't stick around and attack us here is because they were afraid some other coaches might come along as well."

"That means they're going to be waiting up ahead, doesn't it?" Jordan asked.

"Yeah, that would sure be my guess," Quince said, nodding his head. "The question is . . . what are you going to do about it?"

"Well, I don't rightly know," Jordan admitted, stroking his cheek. "I reckon I'm just going to have to give this a little thought." Folding his arms across his broad chest, Will Jordan stared off into the distance, his eyes unfocused, as he considered their dilemma.

Chapter Thirteen

By the time the bodies were buried and the horses watered and fed, Rachel came out to announce that supper, which consisted of fried salt pork, biscuits, and gravy, was ready.

"Sorry about the fare, gentlemen, but this is all we could find," Kate apologized as the men filed into the station building.

"It smells awfully good to me," Quince remarked, and the others concurred, except for Matthews, who grumbled sourly.

As they all sat down to the meal, Jordan called for their attention. When everyone grew quiet, he began to speak.

"I'd like to talk some things over with you folks. Judging from the track that Quince spotted, it's more'n likely that Deekus Tombs and his bunch were the ones who murdered the men here, meaning it's likely they know about the money. It's also possible that they're figuring on hitting us tonight while we're all sleepin' here at the way station."

"We goin' to post a guard?" Beans asked.

"Well, we could do that," Jordan replied. He paused for a moment. "Or, we could go on ahead."

"You mean keep on driving right through the night?" Gib asked.

"Yes. I know the horses are tired. Can they do it?"

"Well, I s'pose they could if we don't have to run 'em any."

Jordan shook his head. "I can't promise you that we won't have to run them," he said. "Deekus and his bunch could be waiting for us."

"Yes, well, that's not the only problem we'll be facing," Gib said. "The trail gets a little more hazardous from here on, twisting alongside steep drop-offs and the like. It would be much more dangerous at night. If just one of the horses stumbles, they could pull us over the side. And in some of those places the fall could be five or six hundred feet."

"Do I have a say in this?" Damon asked.

" 'Course you do. We all do," Jordan replied.

"I'm concerned about Lucy," Damon said. He nodded toward one of the rooms where Lucy was lying in bed. "I'm afraid that the longer we delay, the more dangerous it will be for her. Staying the entire night here might be too long for her. We need to get her to a doctor as quickly as we can."

"Well, then, that settles it. I'm for going on," Kate said.

"So am I," Rachel added.

"So you are suggesting that we put all our lives in danger, just because this . . . this gambler says we should go on?" Matthews spoke up. "You heard what the driver said. Traveling over these roads at night is dangerous, whether Deekus Tombs is out there waiting for us or not. I think we should stay right here tonight."

"No, the sheriff is right," Quince said. "If we stay here, we are just sitting ducks for Tombs. It's best that we go on. The least we can do is make ourselves moving targets. Besides, he wouldn't expect us to go on tonight so even if he is waiting for us, he probably wouldn't be set up until tomorrow."

"That's just great," Matthews said sarcastically. "First we hear from a gambler, then from a criminal. Of course, I suppose we should pay some attention to him as to how one goes about robbing a stagecoach. After all, he is the only one of us who has any experience."

"It wasn't a stagecoach, it was a bank. And he didn't do it," Rachel said.

Quince looked toward Rachel in pleasant surprise, and Rachel held his stare.

"How do you know he didn't do it?"

"Because he told me he didn't do it," Rachel said, simply.

"Great Caesar's ghost," Matthews snorted. "Am I the only one of this entire bunch who hasn't taken leave of his senses? After all, it's the money I'm carrying that Deekus Tombs is after. That means I have the most to lose of any of us, and I demand that we stay."

"You're right when you say that the money you are carrying is the cause of our problems—that, and your obvious big mouth in letting everyone know about it. But we could all lose our lives," Jordan said. "So that doesn't give you any bigger a stake than anyone else. I say that we put it to a vote. All who are in favor of going ahead, raise their hand."

Everyone around the table raised their hands, including Gib and Beans. Then, reluctantly, Matthews raised his hand as well.

"Well, that makes it unanimous. I'm glad to see that you switched your vote, Mr. Matthews," Jordan said.

"I am not opposed to going on. After all, I have an obligation to the people who are waiting for this money. Regardless of what you may think of me, Sheriff, I am a banker and I hold that responsibility very seriously. I just wanted to make certain that everyone considered all the possibilities, that's all."

"Very good. We'll push on ahead, then."

"Will, I have a suggestion," Quince offered.

"All right, let's hear it."

Putting down his fork, the young rancher said, "The regular stage road goes along the west side of the mountains, along the Belle Fourche River. Suppose we cut through at Bear Pass, then go up the east side of the mountains, along Lodgepole Creek. Tombs and his men won't be looking for us over there."

"I know the road you are talking about," Gib said, slowly rubbing the stubble on his chin as he considered Quince's recommendation. "I've been that way on horseback a couple of times. I don't know if we can get a stage through there or not."

"Sure we can," Quince insisted. "Two years ago, my brother and I took a loaded wagon up that trail. Gib, you are a better driver than either Cole or I was. If we could get that wagon through, I know you can take the stage through."

"It's up to you Gib," Jordan said. "Quince is right, Tombs definitely won't be looking for us east of the mountains."

Gib took a sip of his coffee, then nodded. "All right, Will, if you want to try that way, I'm game."

"There's a problem neither one of you is considerin'," Beans pointed out, his words muffled by the food in his mouth.

"What's that?" Gib asked.

"Well, sir, we ain't changin' the team here, so that means that if we go up the east side, we ain't' goin' to be able to change the team at the next station, neither. That means we won't be able to change the team again for the whole rest of the way. The coach can maybe make it through the trail, but can the horses make it? They may get so plumb tuckered out that they just drop right in their harness."

"Not if we baby them as much as possible," Quince suggested. "Gib, suppose we leave all the luggage here locked up in the storeroom, and send a wagon back for it later. We'll take only a few necessities, including whatever food and cooking utensils we can rustle up here. And when we have a pretty steep grade, all the passengers can help things along by getting out and walking."

"That might work," Gib admitted.

"Wait a minute! Hold on here!" Ethan Matthews interjected. "I'm against all this."

"I thought you voted to go on ahead," Jordan said.

"Yes, after some expressed reservations, I did vote to go on ahead. But I thought we were going to proceed by the regular route." Matthews looked at Quince through narrowed eyes. "Now this man comes up with the wild suggestion that we go up the other side of the mountains, by a route that our driver is not familiar with, and even you suggest might be too difficult a transit for the coach. I say we stop and think this over for a while. I mean, what do we really know about this man? We know that he was convicted for robbery. We know that he escaped prison, and suddenly appeared on the trail this morning to conveniently get himself in among us. I think it is very likely that he is in cahoots with that gang of thieves and cutthroats, and now he's just trying to set us up for an ambush. If we go up the east side of the mountains, there won't be anyone we can turn to for help."

Jordan stared at the stiff little man. "If Tombs and his bunch hit us out on the trail, there won't be anyone we can turn to for help, no matter which side of the mountains we're on," the lawman said. "And if they're looking for us on the west side, then the east side is our best bet."

"Unless, of course, this man has arranged for them to be waiting for us on the other side."

Sighing impatiently, Jordan remarked, "I have known Quince Fremont for a long time. I believed him when he told me he was set-up by Deekus Tombs. And I believe him now when he says he overheard them planning to hold up this stage. And I don't believe he would try and set the rest of us up for an ambush. He's not the kind of man who could do something like that."

"So the rest of us have to put our lives in jeopardy because you believe him?" Matthews asked.

Jordan turned to the stage driver. "All right, Gib, I'm going to put you on the spot. Do we take Quince's suggestion to go up the east side or not? After all, you are the one who has to drive."

"I've know Quince about as long as you have, and I don't believe he's in with that bunch, either. And since Tombs is most likely waitin' for us up along the Belle Fourche somewhere, then I say we go up Lodgepole Creek."

"Beans?" Jordan asked.

Beans sopped up the last of the gravy from his plate with a piece of biscuit. He spoke just before he put it in his mouth.

"I'm paid to ride shotgun, Sheriff, not to make no decisions. You fellas want to take this here coach to China, well I reckon I'll be sittin' up there on the box the whole way. Long as I get paid, that is."

"Sheriff, may I raise a concern?" Damon asked.

"Go ahead."

"We have a sick little girl with us. She needs to get into a town as quickly as possible. Now, which way is faster?"

"The Belle Fourche route is the fastest, by perhaps half a day. Maybe more," Gib said.

"Then, for the girl's sake, perhaps we should

take that route . . . or at least give her mother the option of being the deciding factor."

"Mrs. O'Leary," Jordan asked. "Do you want to go the Belle Fourche route, which is the faster? Or the Lodgepole route, which we believe has less chance of running into Deekus Tombs?"

"I want to go the way he suggested," Kate said, nodding toward Quince.

"Even though it's slower?" Jordan asked.

"Yes," Kate answered emphatically. "Sheriff Jordan, surely you remember that horrible incident a couple of years ago when they found a rancher, his wife, and their little girl and boy murdered? Everyone says that Deekus Tombs is the one who did it. I don't know if he did it or not, but I'm not anxious to expose Lucy to that kind of danger. Going this way might mean Lucy is sick for a bit longer before she sees a doctor, but I'd rather her be sick than dead." She shuddered slightly, adding, "And if Deekus Tombs finds us, I'm afraid that's what we will all be."

"Then it's decided," Will announced. "We'll go by way of the Lodgepole Creek road."

"Beans," Gib said, wiping his mouth with a napkin and getting up from the table, "what say you and me go outside and start unloadin' the luggage? We need to get it as light as we can."

"Anybody gonna eat this last biscuit an' piece

of meat?'' Beans asked, pointing toward the platter. When no one answered, he made a sandwich and then took a bite of it as he quickly followed Gib out the door.

Jordan stood and walked around to Quince. "We won't be needin' these things anymore," he said, unlocking Quince's handcuffs.

"What?" Ethan Matthews sputtered angrily. "Just what do you think you are doing?"

"Look, if Quince is lying to us, if he really is setting us up for an ambush, then it's too late. We've already taken the bait. On the other hand, if he's tellin' the truth, we're goin' to need every gun we've got. It's time to make the decision one way or the other as to whether we can trust him, and I've made that decision."

"Without asking us?"

"I'm the only lawman on the coach. I'm the one charged with making the decision," Jordan said.

"You'll certainly get no objections from me," Damon said.

"The more guns we have, the safer I'll feel," Kate added.

"I can't believe this!" Matthews sputtered. "You people actually trust this man?"

"I trust him completely," Rachel said.

Smiling, Quince nodded toward the other passengers. "I thank you for your vote of confidence," he said.

Angrily, Matthews stormed out of the building, slamming the door behind him.

"You're going to need this as well," Jordan told the young prisoner, handing Quince his revolver. He shoved a dozen slugs out of his own gun belt and handed them over. Quince pushed six of them into empty slots on his own belt, then loaded the other six into the cylinder of the revolver.

"Beans tells me there's an extra rifle, too," Jordan said.

His blue eyes regarding the lawman intently, Quince smiled and replied softly, "Thanks, Will, I won't let you down."

"Didn't figure you to," the sheriff replied.

The sound of a shot rolled down the mountainside, then echoed back from the neighboring mountains. With the pistol in his hand still smoking, Hawk turned to the others with a smile on his face. He had just broken a tossed whiskey bottle with his marksmanship.

"I'd like to see anyone beat that," he said.

Hawk was the youngest of all Deekus Tombs's men. Just over twenty, he was dressed in jeans and a stained collarless shirt. His chin bristled with irregular patches of beard and his eyes were like those of a snake: small, dark, beady, and piercing. He sometimes told people he was from Texas, though in fact he was the son of an Ohio preacher.

"Pretty impressive," Deekus agreed.

"Pretty impressive? I'll bet there's not more'n one man out of a hundred who can do that!"

"You might be right," Deekus said.

"What about you, Silver? You think you could do it?"

"I doubt it."

"What about you, Prescott?"

Clint Prescott, who was the oldest of the group, spit a stream of tobacco juice out before he answered. "Don't reckon I could," he said.

Hawk twirled his pistol on his finger before slipping it back in his holster. "Didn't think any of you could," he said. "Don't know where you boys would be without me."

" 'Course . . . the whiskey bottle don't shoot back," Deekus said.

"Maybe not, but them folks in Theresa was sure shootin' back, an' by God, I killed me a couple there," Hawk said.

"How do you know?" Prescott asked. "There was so much shootin' goin' on that nobody knows who killed who."

"Well, since I'm the best shot of all of us, I figure that I'm the one that got nearly all of them."

"If you say so," Deekus said.

Hawk Peters pulled his pistol out and began

reloading it. "Say, Deekus, you reckon there'll be any women on that stage?"

"Could be. There almost always is."

Hawk rubbed himself. "That's good," he said. "If there are, I might just show them a good time."

"Like you showed that rancher's wife a good time last year?" Prescott asked.

"That crazy woman," Hawk said. "All she would'a had to do was just lay there an' enjoy it till it was over. Instead, she tried to grab my gun. It was almost like she was wantin' me to kill her."

Prescott chuckled. "Maybe she would rather be killed than have anything to do with you. I mean, you aren't the handsomest critter who ever—"

Before Prescott could finish his statement, Hawk had the barrel of his gun resting on Prescott's upper lip just below his nose. "Well, now," he said, slowly cocking his gun. The cylinder turned with a metallic click. "I suppose you think all the women think you're good looking? We'll just have to see what they think about you once I blow your nose off your face."

Deekus raised his arm and a small pistol popped into his hand from its concealed position up his sleeve. He put the small gun to Hawk's temple.

"Put away your gun, Hawk," Deekus said easily.

Hawk laughed. "Haw! What do you think you're goin' to do to me with that little pepper box?"

"I can put a little bullet in your little brain," Deekus answered coldly.

Hawk held his pistol on Prescott for a moment longer. "I can kill him before you pull the trigger."

"Go ahead," Deekus said.

"What?"

"Go ahead, kill him. It don't mean nothin' to me," Deekus said. "But if you pull that trigger, I'm going to kill you."

"Why? This ain't got nothin' to do with you," Hawk complained.

"Yeah, it does," Deekus answered. "Ever since the two Pogue boys got themselves killed, I've just barely had enough men to get the job done. If you kill Clint here, then killin' you wouldn' make things any worse."

Hawk held his pistol to Prescott's lip for a moment longer.

"Look, if we're going to do this thing, let's commence the killin' and be done with it," Deekus said. "I'll count to three. If you ain't put your gun away by then, I'm just goin' to kill you, whether you pull the trigger or not."

Hawk lowered his gun, then smiled. "I wasn't

really goin' to kill him," he said. "I was just havin' some fun with him."

"Too bad," Deekus said. " 'Cause I was goin' to kill you, and have fun doin' it."

"Come on, fellas. That ain't the kind of fun we ought to be thinkin' about anyway," Silver said. "The kind of fun to think about is the kind we're going to have after we hit the stage. How much did you say is there, Deekus?"

"Over one hundred thousand dollars," Deekus replied. After Hawk holstered his pistol, Deekus let the little derringer slip back up in to his sleeve.

"How much is that for each of us?" Silver asked.

"It'll be ten thousand a piece."

"Ten thousand for each . . . Wait a minute, that's only thirty thousand dollars," Hawk said. "That leaves you seventy thousand."

"No it don't," Deekus said.

"What do you mean, it don't? Thirty thousand from one hundred thousand leaves seventy thousand dollars."

"It ain't all for me," Deekus insisted. "I got expenses. Plus, how do you think we found out about this money shipment?" Deekus tapped his finger on his temple. "We found out about it 'cause I got someone on the inside."

"Yeah? Who?" Hawk asked.

Deekus shook his head. "All you need to

know is that I got someone working for us, and it's worth ten thousand dollars to each of you."

"Hey, Clint, what you going to do with your ten thousand dollars?" Silver asked.

"I'm going to get me a woman and a bottle of champagne," Prescott answered.

Silver laughed. "Champagne? Why?"

" 'Cause I ain't never had me any, that's why," Prescott replied, as if that were reason enough.

Chapter Fourteen

It had been a long time since anyone had used the Lodgepole Creek road, and the route, though passable, was extremely difficult. At one point the stage lurched so sharply to the left that everyone inside was thrown against each other or the sides of the stagecoach. Lucy cried out in pain and Kate comforted her as best she could, although her eyes reflected her own concern.

"We were absolute fools to come this way!" Ethan Matthews shouted.

"We all agreed that this was the way we were going to come, Mr. Matthews," Rachel pointed out.

"But I believe I made it perfectly clear that I was agreeing with reservations." Matthews held up his finger. "With reservations, madam," he reemphasized.

"You got on the coach, Mr. Matthews," Damon said. "By that action, you removed your reservations."

"I do not agree with your premise, sir," Matthews said in a haughty tone.

"Whoa!" Gib Crabtree called from his seat on the box. The coach lurched to a sudden stop.

"Now what?" Matthews asked, his growing irritation making him more and more unpleasant to be around.

Quince Fremont, who had been riding on top of the coach, climbed down and dropped to the ground. Opening the door, he announced, "Folks, I'm afraid you're all going to have to get out and walk for a bit. There's a pretty steep grade coming up, and we're going to need to lighten the coach."

Damon stepped out of the coach first. Turning to help the others, he held out his hand to prevent Lucy from getting out when the little girl appeared in the doorway. "I think it would be best if you stayed in the coach, honey," he told her kindly. "You don't weigh enough to make that much difference, and you shouldn't be walking."

"Do you think it would be all right, Quince?" Kate asked, poking her head out the doorway over her daughter's shoulder.

"Sure," Quince replied. "Mr. Parker is right. Lucy doesn't weigh much."

"I can walk," Lucy insisted. "I'm not a baby."

"I know you're not a baby, Lucy," the young

rancher replied. "That's why I think you could do something for me, if you would."

"What's that?"

"Well, somebody has to stay inside and keep an eye on things for us in there. Since you weigh the least, I was sort of hoping you would do it. You can even lie down while you're doing it."

"Oh. Sure, all right, I'll do that," Lucy agreed. Her face was sallow and her eyes were slightly glazed as she moved back into the coach and laid back down.

When Matthews got out, he looked up at the driver's seat where Gib sat holding the reins. "Mr. Crabtree, just so that you fully understand, I want you to know that I shall be writing a letter to the Wyoming Coach and Express Company demanding a refund of my fare. I paid to *ride* to Antelope Springs, not *walk*."

"Yes, sir," Gib replied. "I'm sure you'll be writing to the company with all kinds of complaints. From what I can tell, you don't ever seem to run out of 'em."

"And I'll add surliness to my list of complaints as well," Matthews promised, shaking his finger angrily. "There's no excuse for you to be discourteous to your passengers."

"I reckon not," Gib replied. His voice sounded amused. "Now, if I ask you just real polite, would you please get you narrow little ass around to the rear of the coach along with all the other passengers?''

Sniffing derisively, the bank clerk did as he was asked, clutching his satchel protectively to his thin chest.

With everyone walking along behind the coach, the driver whistled to the team, and they started up the grade. It was a long, gradual climb, and the coach moved no faster than the passengers could walk. Finally they reached the top of the hill, and Gib halted the horses to give them a few minutes to rest, then he informed the passengers that they could reboard.

It was late enough in the day now that the western sky was ablaze with color. Rachel Kincaid was watching the sunset through the window on her side of the coach, and she exclaimed to her friend, ''Oh, Kate, would you look at that beautiful sky? How could I have ever let the beauty of this wild, rugged country slip away from me? Boston has much to offer, I'll admit . . . but it has nothing to compare with all this.''

Kate chuckled. ''Is this the same Rachel Kincaid who was on the train with me? The young woman who was so resentful of having been brought back and who could hardly wait to convince her father that the only sensible thing for him to do was sell his ranch and move to Boston?"

"There have been a few changes in the way I look at things since then," Rachel admitted, her face flushing slightly.

Kate reached over and squeezed her hand. "I'm glad to hear that," she said. "You and your ma and pa are good people, Rachel, and if we are ever to make anything of this place out here, it's going to be because we have a lot of people like you and your family."

The coach hit another bump at that moment and Lucy gave a sharp little cry.

"Mrs. O'Leary," Damon said quietly. "Perhaps she would be more comfortable if you loosened her clothing. That would take some of the pressure off her stomach."

"Yes," Kate agreed. "Yes, I'm sure that's a good idea. I hadn't thought of that." She started to loosen Lucy's dress, but the girl put her hand down to stop her.

"No, Mama," she complained. "What if my dress falls off and people laugh at me."

"Honey, your dress isn't going to fall off," Kate said. "I'll make sure of that."

"And besides, if anyone happened to laugh at you, I would put them in jail," Jordan offered.

"You promise?"

"I promise."

"All right," Lucy agreed solemnly. "You can loosen my dress, Mama."

"How does your stomach feel now, Lucy?" Damon asked, his concern evident.

"That does make it feel better," Lucy told him. "But it still hurts something awful."

Kate smoothed back the girl's hair. "We'll be in Antelope Springs before too much longer now. And the moment we get there, I'll take you to see Dr. Presnell. He isn't like the man we saw last night."

"I hope not," Lucy said quietly. "He was awful and he didn't help at all."

"Shhh," Kate said easily. "You go to sleep now. That's the best thing for you."

"Yes, Mama." Lucy closed her eyes and within a few minutes was breathing rhythmically.

"I had almost forgotten about old Doc Presnell," Rachel said. "I'm surprised that he is still alive, much less still practicing medicine."

"I think he would like to retire," Kate replied. "But there is no one around to take his place and he doesn't want to leave the town in the lurch. That poor, wonderful old man is going to work until the day he dies, I'm afraid."

"Still, it's lucky that we have him. It's lucky that we have any kind of doctor, I suppose."

From his seat on the roof, Quince Fremont listened to the conversations going on inside the coach. Quince believed that what he had missed most while being in prison were the little things that everyone takes for granted when they have their freedom. He had almost forgotten how pleasurable it was just to have a quiet talk with a good friend without having a guard watching, thinking you were planning something. How he had missed just walking in the woods, feeling the springy softness of pine needles underfoot while listening to the song birds. Or the simple pleasure derived from sitting in a porch swing, moving lazily while watching the sunset.

When the coach had to be emptied again a half hour later, Quince hopped down and walked directly behind it. Rachel dawdled about ten yards behind the others, taking in the beauty of the mountains. Quince dropped back to walk alongside her.

"I can't tell you how good it is to see you again," he told her, keeping pace with her.

"Why?" she asked.

"Why? Well, because you . . ." He paused. How could he tell her that, while in prison, he had fantasies about her, of moments exactly like this one. He couldn't tell her that there were times when he wondered if he would ever see any young woman again. "You were someone that I wanted desperately to believe that I was innocent."

"But I was already in Boston when all this

happened," Rachel replied. "The only reason I knew anything about it at all was because Papa sent me the newspaper clippings."

Quince sighed. "Ah, yes, the newspaper clippings. I never figured I would get my name in the paper for any reason. And now it's plastered in newspapers everywhere, and not for anything good."

"If it is any comfort to you, Mama and Papa never believed you and Cole were guilty," Rachel said. "And neither did I."

"That makes me feel good," Quince said.

"Is it . . . is it awful in prison?" Rachel asked.

Quince smiled wryly. "Well, the whole idea of a prison is to make it a place that a person never wants to see again," he explained. "The hope is that after such an unpleasant experience, a man will reform when he gets out rather than do something that will send him back."

"Does it work?"

"I don't know," Quince answered, sighing. "Maybe it does, sometimes. But most of the time I think it just makes men harder. I'm not saying that people like Deekus Tombs don't deserve to go to prison—or hang, for that matter—I'm just saying that the experience inside a prison generally makes a man worse than when he went in."

"But it didn't make you worse," Rachel offered, touching Quince's arm briefly. "You are as nice now as you were when I left for Boston."

"I don't understand. If you felt that way, why were you so . . . ?" he let the question hang.

"Why was I what?"

"Standoffish," Quince said.

"Standoffish? Why, whatever do you mean by that, Quince Fremont?"

"At the cattlemen's ball, you wouldn't meet my gaze," Quince said. "And every time I walked over to try and start a conversation with you, you would move away."

"Yes," Rachel admitted.

"Then it was intentional? You really were trying to avoid me?"

"Yes."

"Why, this . . . this is incredible," Quince said. "I had no idea that you would so readily admit to avoiding me."

"Why shouldn't I admit it? That's exactly what I was doing. In fact, Mr. Fremont, you were responsible in no small part for my going to Boston."

Quince shook his head. "Well, now, I don't understand that at all. Was I ever rude to you? Did I ever say or do something that displeased you?"

"You were never rude to me, but you did do something that displeased me."

"What was it?" He held up his hand. "If my right hand offends thee, I shall cut it off."

"It wasn't your right arm. It was your left."

"My left arm did something? Rachel, what ever are you talking about?"

"I'm talking about her."

"Her? Who? There is no other woman. There never has been another woman."

"I saw you with her."

"Rachel, you aren't making sense, girl. I don't know what you saw, or thought you saw, but there is no other woman."

"Once, just before the cattlemen's ball, I went into town to pick up a few things. You didn't see me, but I saw you. I was sitting in a wagon in front of Dunnigan's store, and I saw you escorting a woman into the Last Chance Saloon."

Quince shook his head. "I don't recall anything like that," he said.

"See, that's why I've never said anything about it before now. I knew you would deny it, yet I saw you with my own eyes."

"Who was the woman?"

"Well, she was certainly no one I would ever encounter socially. But I don't know how you could forget her . . . the way she was dressed, the yellow hair piled on top of her head, the—"

Suddenly Quince began to laugh.

"What is it? Why are you laughing?"

"You're talking about Rosie," he said.

"Rosie? So, you do remember her."

"Of course I remember her. Rachel, Rosie is a

saloon hall girl. She was going into the Last Chance Saloon because she works there."

"You were escorting her."

"Yes, I suppose I was. I probably ran into her on the street," Quince said. "And since we were both going there, I offered her my arm."

"But, how could you let yourself be seen with such a creature?" Rachel asked.

"Because, whether she is a soiled dove or not, she is still a woman," Quince replied. "And I am, by inclination, courteous to all women. But don't let the fact that I am courteous to other women bother you, Rachel."

"Bother me? Why should it bother me?"

"I don't know why, but it obviously does," Quince said. He smiled, broadly, then added, "But I'm glad that it does."

"Quince Fremont, you are making absolutely no sense at all."

"I'm making sense all right. And you know it."

"I have no idea what you are talking about," Rachel said.

"I'm talking about us."

"Us? There is no us."

"In my imagination there is. A man gets a lot of time to think when he's in prison. And a lot of my thoughts were of you." Quince chuckled.

"Why are you laughing?"

"I was just wondering . . . while you were in Boston, going to concerts and museums, and being received in polite society, what you would have thought if you realized that, back in a dark, dank cell in a Wyoming prison, some creature who was barely hanging onto a shred of humanity was thinking about you?"

"May I make a confession?" Rachel responded. "Once, at the ballet, one of the dancers reminded me of you. I began thinking of you and it wasn't until I heard the applause of the audience that I knew the performance was over." She smiled up at him. "You ruined the entire ballet for me," she said.

Quince's chuckle turned into whoops of laughter. "A ballet dancer? A ballet dancer reminded you of me?"

"Well, he was quite handsome," Rachel protested. Then, quickly, she covered her mouth with her hand. "Not meaning that you are handsome," she added, then realizing that was wrong stammered, "Not that you *aren't* handsome, I mean you are, but . . ."

Finally, with her cheeks flaming in embarrassment, Rachel walked away from him, hurrying all the way up to the front of the coach.

The others wondered why Quince was laughing so hard, but upon seeing Rachel's reaction to it, decided that it would be best not to ask.

When they reached the top of the grade, Gib

let his horses rest again. By now the sun had set, and it was quite dark over half of the sky. The passengers had already decided that they were not going to try to push through all night. However, Gib did have a particular place in mind where he wanted to make camp, and that was another five miles or so ahead. He had camped there when he rode through once before. It was a grassy glen in a little valley, where they would have water and some shelter against the cold night wind.

Beans was tending to the horses, and seeing him standing alone near the head of the team, Quince walked up to him. He had been looking for the opportunity to speak with the shotgun guard alone, and now he looked around to make certain no one was close enough to overhear them.

"Where were you in prison, Beans?" Quince asked without preamble.

Surprised, Beans gasped and looked up at him sharply. "What? Who . . . who told you I was ever in prison?" he demanded.

"Why, you did."

"Me? I never did no such thing! What makes you think I told you that?"

"There's a look a person gets when he's been inside," Quince explained. "That look never goes away, no matter how long ago it was. You have that look, my friend."

Beans was quiet for a long moment; then he glanced back at the others. Finally, he let out a long sigh. "Yeah," he said. "I reckon I know about that look." Unconsciously, he fingered the long, disfiguring scar that slashed across his face.

"Is that where you got that scar? In prison?"

"Yeah. Please don't say nothin' about it, Quince. Nobody else knows, and if the company found out, I'd most likely lose my job. I can't see the Wyoming Coach and Express Company hirin' a man who once served time for robbin' a stage. And it's awful hard trying to go straight if you ain't got no job."

"I surely do see your point," Quince replied. "When were you in?"

"About five years ago," the bandy-legged guard answered.

"Here in Wyoming?"

"No. It was back in Kansas."

"Kansas? Deekus Tombs was in the state prison back in Kansas about five years ago, wasn't he?"

Beans's eyes narrowed, and he nodded cautiously.

"You met him there, didn't you?" Quince guessed.

Looking at him warily, Beans replied, "Yeah, I did. Fact is, Deekus Tombs was my cellmate."

* * *

While the others took the opportunity to leave the wagon road and walk into the surrounding woods to refresh themselves, Damon Parker ambled over to talk to Kate O'Leary, who was looking in through the coach window at her daughter.

"Are you doing all right?" Damon asked, gauging her carefully.

"Yes, I'm doing just fine, thank you," Kate answered, smiling back at him. She nodded toward the inside of the stage. "I wish I could say the same for Lucy, poor thing."

"Is she sleeping now?"

"Yes."

"Well, that's the best thing for her at the moment," Damon advised. "If she's asleep, she's totally relaxed, and the more relaxed she is, the less strain she's going to feel." Sticking his hand in through the open window, he felt Lucy's face. "She's still fevered," he said. "Although, for the moment, it doesn't seem to be out of hand."

Kate cocked her head and stared at him for a long moment, then she said, "Sheriff Jordan is right. You really do have a feel for doctoring, don't you?"

"Well, I thought I did, once," the gambler answered without elaboration.

"Maybe you should be a doctor."

Damon smiled at her sadly. "No, I'm afraid I can't agree with you there."

They were both silent for a moment, then Damon said, "Tell me about this man in Antelope Springs, your doctor there. I believe you said his name was Presnell?"

"Yes, Robert Presnell. He's an older man who has experienced just about everything. He was an army surgeon during the war, and he's certainly done his share of removing bullets and repairing broken bones and such. I believe he's a very good doctor, and he's pulled a lot of folks through some pretty bad times."

"Do you have faith in him?"

"Yes."

"Then that's the most important thing," Damon remarked. "And if you want my opinion, I would say that you are very lucky that the doctor back in Millersburg did nothing for Lucy but prescribe a purgative."

"A useless purgative."

An acrimonious look came over the gambler's face. "If it was just useless, that wouldn't be so bad. In Lucy's case, the doctor's purgative may even have been harmful. I strongly recommend that you throw the bottle away."

"I already did," Kate admitted.

Damon smiled. "That's good."

"You've been most kind to look after Lucy as you have, Mr. Parker. And I would like to thank you."

"Please, we have shared so much of this journey now. Don't you think you could call me Damon?"

Kate laughed. "If I call you Damon, the next thing you know, Lucy will be calling you Damon."

Damon laughed with her. "Well, that wouldn't be so bad, would it? She seems to be a very bright and well-mannered girl . . . someone I wouldn't mind knowing." He paused and looked down at her. "As a matter of fact," he continued, his voice tender, "I don't mind admitting to you that I would also like to know her mother better."

Kate's face was filled with surprise. She looked away, clearly nonplussed.

"I'm sorry. I didn't mean to make you uncomfortable," Damon said softly.

Looking back at him, she gave him a small smile. "That's all right. The truth is, I guess I'd like to know you better as well. You're a most interesting person."

"You know what I mean, Kate," Damon said quietly.

For a long moment Kate and Damon looked at each other. Without thinking, the gambler reached out and stroked Kate's hair, telling her, "Your hair is so beautiful. I've noticed that when the sun strikes it, it almost looks as though it is on fire." He smiled knowingly. "It seems most appropriate, because I get the feeling you are a fiery woman, Kate O'Leary."

Kate laughed, and Damon instinctively leaned toward her until their lips were but a breath apart. His hand moved to her shoulder, then to the back of her neck, running over her soft, warm skin. Putting his arms around her, Damon gently urged Kate's body against his. He bent his head, and for a brief moment their lips touched.

Then Kate suddenly pulled away and stepped back, and the gambler inwardly sighed. He knew that the beautiful woman standing an arm's length away from him had been longing for him as much as he had been longing for her, and he was startled by the depth of his feelings for her. It had been a long time since he had allowed himself to be close to a woman in anything more than a purely physical way . . . no one, in fact, since Deborah.

Kate was staring at him, and he could almost feel the struggle within her. "Kate," he whispered, his voice hoarse.

Kate shook her head and then looked around to make certain no one had seen them. "We . . . we shouldn't have done that."

Damon wondered how much of her hesitation was because he was a gambler, which was not exactly the most respectable of professions. He also wondered whether, if he altered his way of living, she would find him suitable.

Damon was about to speak when Gib Crabtree called from the other side of the stage. "Okay, folks! Let's get back on the coach. We've got about five miles to go before we make camp for the night."

I may surprise you, Kate O'Leary, Damon thought as he helped the beautiful redhead back onto the coach. *And I may surprise myself as well.*

Chapter Fifteen

On a trail alongside the Belle Fourche River on the opposite side of the mountains from the old, abandoned road the coach was taking, Deekus Tombs and his men waited. The stage had been scheduled to pass about two hours before sunset, and though it was not yet completely dark, the sun was down and the stage still had not shown.

Clint Prescott walked over to a yucca plant and began relieving himself.

"What you doin' there, Prescott? Floodin' the valley?" Silver asked to the amusement of the others.

"Nah, he's just waterin' the lilies is all," Hawk suggested.

Finishing, Prescott buttoned his pants and turned toward the others. "Seems to me like you boys could think of somethin' a little more serious to be concerned about than me takin' a piss," he grumbled.

"Like what?"

"Like, where the hell is the stagecoach?" he asked. "We been hangin' around here practically all day."

"It'll be here," Deekus said.

"That's what you been sayin' for hours," Prescott complained. "Hell, there ain't no stage comin' through this way. If there was, it woulda been here by now."

"Maybe Clint's right. Could be the stage ain't comin'," Silver suggested.

Deekus Tombs spit a stream of tobacco into the dirt, then wiped his mouth with the back of his hand. "If the stage comes every other time, just what the hell makes you think it won't be comin' this time?" he asked.

"Well, for one thing, we killed them people back at the way station," Silver said. "Maybe we ought not to have done that."

"What would you have done? Leave 'em alive so's they could warn the stage about us?"

"What I'm sayin' is, maybe we done just that anyhow," Silver suggested. "If they got there and seen ever'body dead, don't you think they might get just a bit suspicious?"

"I don't know," Deekus admitted. "Could be you're right. I been studyin' on that myself." He sighed, and stroked his chin. "All right, I'll tell you what we can do. Let's ride back along the trail and see if we can find out what happened to them."

"How far back do we go?"

"Hell, as far back as we need to go. All the way to the way station if we need to."

"You really want to go there? We left three dead men there."

"So what? They wasn't no problem to handle when they was alive. You think they're goin' to bother us now that they're dead?"

"It ain't that. It's just that . . . well, what if there's someone there askin' questions?" Silver asked.

"If they ask the wrong questions, we'll kill them," Deekus answered simply. "But I aim to find out what's happened to that damned stagecoach."

From his seat, Gib pointed to a grassy area between the road and a fast-running stream. "The place I was thinking we might camp is just down there, at the bottom of this hill," he said. He paused for a moment, then added, "But it looks to me like there's been some road washout or somethin'. I sure don't remember the road bein' all this narrow. Getting down there's not goin' to be easy. Hell, it might not even be possible."

Descending rather steeply for about three hundred yards downhill from the coach, the road curved sharply to the right and then narrowed to the barest sliver of a path.

Setting the brake on the stage, Gib and Beans walked down for a closer look at the road they would have to traverse. They stayed there for a long time, talking and gesturing, and finally Jordan, Quince, and Damon walked down to join them.

Jordan asked the question that was on everyone's mind. "What do you think? Can we make it through here all right?"

"Not any way I can figure," Gib answered. "In fact, unless there's another route through here that I don't know about, we're just about stumped." Turning to the young rancher, Gib asked, "What about it, Quince? You got any ideas?"

"No, I don't," Quince replied, glumly. Folding his arms across his chest, he studied the road. "I swear, Gib, I don't remember this road being this narrow anywhere."

"I don't, either," Gib replied. "But it could be some of it got washed out in the spring runoff. You take the rains and the thaw, and sometimes you wind up with a real gully washer. And if the road ain't bein' used regular, why, it can start crumblin' away without anyone knowin' anything about it."

"I guess it don't matter if that's the case or not, 'cause it looks like we got no choice but to turn around and go back," Gib said.

"Wait a minute," Damon put in. "Are you

saying now that we are going to have to double back and go up the other side of this mountain range, just the way we originally planned?"

"I reckon that is what I'm sayin', seein' as I don't figure we got any other choice," Gib said.

"If we go back that way, how long will that delay our getting to Antelope Springs?" Damon asked.

"It'll set us back a day for sure. Maybe as much as a day and a half."

Damon shook his head. "No, we can't do that. We must get to Antelope Springs with all deliberate speed."

Beans chuckled. "You got some marks picked out there you aim to fleece at the card table, do you?" he asked.

"No," Damon said. "But if we add one more day to our schedule, that sick little girl back there is going to die."

"Whoa! Now hold on there, fella! Where do you get off sayin' somethin' like that? You don't know that."

"Yes, I do."

"This is ridiculous. There's absolutely no way you can know that," Gib insisted.

"Mr. Crabtree, I wish it were otherwise. Please, take my word for it. If we don't get to Antelope Springs in a reasonable length of time that child is going to die. I haven't said anything to her mother because I don't want to alarm her, but I am absolutely certain that Lucy has an inflamed appendix. And if it ruptures, she will die. She may, of course, die anyway, even under a doctor's care, but if we could get her to Antelope Springs and a competent medical practitioner, she would at least have a fighting chance."

"Now, dammit, mister, you can't just come right out and make a statement like that, like maybe you are the high and mighty, or something," Gib said, the tone and tenor of his voice showing his exasperation. "You can't know for sure that that girl's going to die."

"Gib," Jordan said quietly. "For what it's worth, I agree with Mr. Parker. I don't know anything about rupturing appendixes or anything like that, so I can't say what is troubling the girl. But in my time I've seen death on a lot of faces—and I'm seein' it on that little girl's face now. And if you think about it, you'll have to admit that you see it there, too."

"All right, dammit!" Gib said. He sighed. "You're right. It's there. I didn't see it because I didn't want to see it."

"So, what do we do now?" Beans asked.

"We get through," Gib said, matter-of-factly.

"How?" Beans asked.

"I don't know," Gib answered. "And even if we make it to the bottom of this hill, who is to say we won't find another one just as bad, or worse, after this one? But it doesn't matter because somehow, someway, we are going all the way to Antelope Springs."

"Maybe we ought to stay up here tonight," Beans suggested. "Then we can figure out how to tackle this road first thing in the morning."

"No, it ain't goin' to get no easier," Gib said. "We get the coach through this little piece of road first, then we can camp for the night, just like we planned."

Damon studied the road that was causing all the trouble. A sheer rock wall about ten feet high bordered the right side of the road, while on the left there was a sharp drop-off of nearly a hundred feet. Beans measured how wide it was from the wall to the drop-off, finding it almost exactly the same width as the track of the coach wheels. There was a variance of perhaps as little as three inches between staying on the road and dropping the outside wheel rims over the edge. Adding to that was the curve of the road, which meant that as the coach went downhill, it would also have to be turned within the tolerance of that three inches.

"You know, if that coach tumbles over the side and takes the team with it, we're goin' to lose the horses," Gib remarked as he studied the situation. "Then we'd be set afoot out here."

"I know," Jordan said.

"Why don't we disconnect all the horses but one?" Quince suggested. "That way we would only risk one horse."

"Good thinking, Quince," Jordan said. "But maybe we could use two. One in front of the coach and another connected by rope to the rear. That way the horse at the rear could be used to hold the coach back as it starts down the hill."

At that point, Ethan Matthews came down the hill to join them. "Well, it looks as if I was right after all, doesn't it?" he said. "You have no choice now but to go back to the junction of the Belle Fourche River and Lodgepole Creek, then head up the other side of the mountains where there is a decent and passable road."

"We aren't going back," Gib said. "We're goin' through."

"What? You plan to go through here? Why, that's preposterous!" Matthews sputtered. "It's more than preposterous, it's insane! And it's impossible!"

"Thanks for your support and positive outlook, Mr. Matthews," Gib said sarcastically. He looked at the others. "Do any of you have any suggestions?"

"I think I know how we can do it," Damon suggested.

"You!" Matthews hooted. "Oh, that's a good one. First you play doctor, now you are going to play stage driver. Tell me, Mr. Parker, just what makes you think you can drive a stage?"

"Oh, I don't think I *can* drive it," Damon replied. "It takes quite a bit of skill to handle a team and coach like this, and I am convinced that Mr. Crabtree is expert in that field. But I do understand mathematics and geometry. And that is the key that can get us out of here— that is, if you would be interested in hearing it, Mr. Crabtree."

"Sure, let me hear what you've got to say," Gib replied.

"What?" Matthews shouted. "Are you actually going to give credence to this . . . this common saloon hustler? This is absolutely unbelievable! Turn the coach around. Turn it around, I say, and take us over to the other side of the mountains as you were supposed to. I'll not risk this money and my life in some crazy scheme concocted by a confidence man!"

"Well, Mr. Matthews, here's the thing of it," Gib said. "We ain't holdin' you prisoner. If you don't want to ride along with the rest of us in this here coach, why, you're free to get off right here and right now."

Matthews looked around at the distant hills and mountains, vast and empty of any suggestion of civilization other than their own tiny pocket of humanity. "I'd be a fool to start out on my own out here," he retorted. "I've no idea where I am or which way to go. It would be suicide."

"Then you got no choice but to go along with the rest of us," Gib said. "And if you can't say nothin' to help us out, then, damn your hide, don't you say nothin' at all."

"I'm going to remember this, Crabtree," Matthews snapped, pointing his finger at the driver. "I'm going to remember every word you have said to me and every indignity you have put me through. And believe me when I tell you, you will suffer the consequences."

"Oh, I'm sure you will remember, Mr. Matthews," Gib replied in a way that showed that he clearly wasn't concerned. He turned to the gambler. "All right, Mr. Parker, let's hear the mathematical idea."

"Well, it's simple geometry, actually. Here, let me show you," Damon said. He knelt on the ground and then drew a semicircle in the dirt. "Let's say that this arc represents the segment of the road that we now occupy. If we were to carry the arc all the way through, we would have a circle . . . like so." He demonstrated his point by drawing a complete circle. "Now, all we have to do is determine the distance from the arc to the center of the circle. That would be the radius. If we anchored a rope at the radius and tied the other end onto the stage, we could more or less swing the coach around the arc. Even if the outer wheels slipped over the edge, it wouldn't automatically fall, because the rope would keep it in a predetermined arc."

"I'll be damned," Quince said, grinning broadly. "I think you've got something there."

Gib chuckled. "I don't understand half of them words you was sayin', but lookin' at that plan I can tell you it's goin' to work."

Standing, Damon suggested, "If you gentlemen will tie the rope securely to the coach, I'll pace out enough of the road to determine the circle's radius. That way we'll know exactly how long the rope has to be and where to anchor it." He looked at the craggy wall lining one side of the road and added, "It shouldn't be too difficult to find the perfect boulder to use as the anchor."

"Then, let's do it," Jordan suggested, and he, Beans, and Quince started back up the road toward the coach to secure the rope. Damon remained behind, where he began pacing off the road. Periodically he would stop and use his pocket watch to measure the angles he needed to determine the radius.

As soon as the calculations were complete, the plan was put into operation. To the satisfaction and amazement of everyone, the coach, securely anchored by the radius rope, swung around the road as easily as if it had been on a track. At one point, one of the rear wheels slipped over the edge, but the rope held the coach firmly in place, and it was a simple matter to guide the wheel back onto the road to continue.

Whooping with glee, Gib shouted, "Geometry, you say? That there experiment almost makes a body want to go back to school and get more learnin'!"

As they began making camp, Beans remarked to the others, "I tell you what. I can see why that feller's so good at poker. He's about the smartest sumbitch I've ever run across."

After a fire was started, Jordan stood and shouldered a rifle. "We'll split up the watch during the night. I'll go first. Who wants to be second?"

"I have no intention of standing watch," Ethan Matthews declared smugly. "I paid to be a passenger, not a shotgun guard."

"Don't worry about it, Mr. Matthews. I have no intention of asking you to stand watch. I want people I can depend on, not someone who will pee in his pants at the first owl's call."

The men agreed among themselves who would stand watch and in what order. With that decided, the rest of the passengers settled down for the night.

Damon Parker walked over to where Kate O'Leary was sitting beside Lucy. Lucy was sleeping fitfully and Damon knelt beside her, then felt her face. "How is she doing?" he asked, softly.

"Not very well, I'm afraid," Kate answered, shaking her head slowly.

"Kate, I hope I didn't offend you earlier. I certainly wouldn't want to do that."

Kate put her hand on Damon's arm. "It's all right, you don't have to apologize. I wasn't offended."

"Thanks. I worried about that."

"You know, Damon, you may well be the most desirable man I have ever known. But I am a responsible, grown woman. I have a child to raise and a hotel to run. I'm sure that to you, a gambler moving from town to town, and, no doubt getting run out of many of them, my kind of life would be very boring."

"You don't have any idea how unboring that sounds to me right now," Damon said.

"Yes, well, I can't afford to be your experiment, Damon Parker. I hope you can see how it is. As easy as it would be to be swept off my feet by you, it wouldn't do for me to give my heart to a gambler, and especially not now. My only concern at this moment is for my daughter."

Damon nodded slowly. "I understand," he said. "And I want to help in any way that I can."

Tilting her head, she studied him for a long moment before she spoke. "I do believe you mean that. And you have been a great help. I don't know what I would have done without you."

"I wish I could do more," Damon said. He put his hand to Lucy's face, feeling for a temperature.

"She's still running a fever," Kate said.

"Yes, she is." Damon stood up and reached for the water bucket. "I'm going to get some water from the stream. A cold compress on her forehead will bring the temperature down somewhat."

"You're a good man, Damon Parker," Kate said.

Several miles south of where they had waited in vain for the stage, Deekus Tombs and his men reached the confluence of the Belle Fourche and Lodgepole Creek. There, by the light of the full moon, they saw the tracks made by the coach and realized why it had not shown up when it was supposed to.

"Will you look at this?" Deekus shouted angrily. "They went up the west side of the mountains! Now why do you suppose they did that?"

"Probably 'cause somehow they got wind that we're after them," Silver said, his voice full of scorn.

Ignoring the jibe, Deekus smiled broadly. "Well, what do you know? They probably thought they fooled us good. Like as not they're halfway up the valley now, drinkin' coffee and celebratin' how they put one over on old Deekus Tombs. Well, that's good. They'll think they've won now, so they won't be none too alert." He snorted, then added, "Get ready, boys. We're gonna come down on them like a duck on a June bug."

Chapter Sixteen

A cool night breeze glided over the travelers' campsite, though it was so slight that the nearby trees did no more than whisper with its passing. In the distance a coyote barked and was answered by the long plaintive howl of another. Overhead, white stars blazed bright, big, and close.

Quince stood up and walked over to toss another chunk of wood onto the campfire. The fire was kept low so as not to be visible, but Will had decided they could have one as long as they kept it burning low, because they were down in the valley ringed by mountains. To see the fire, an observer would have to be on top of one of the surrounding mountains, though if the flames burned too brightly, its reflection could be seen from quite a distance, even from as far as another mountain range.

After watching the fire for a few moments to make certain it did not flare up, Quince decided to walk down to the edge of the stream. He passed the place where the resting team was tied. Even from this close, they were barely visible, no more than moving shadows within shadows. Standing by the edge of the stream, he looked across the water and into the trees.

A scuffling sound caused him to turn quickly, his gun held at the ready. The tall, solid form of Will Jordan was coming toward him.

"I saw you leave the camp and come down here," the lawman said.

"And you thought maybe I was going to run away?" Quince replied.

"No, nothing like that," Jordan said. Then he smiled. "Well, maybe I did give it some thought. Don't know as I would blame you too much if you did."

"If I wanted to get away, Will, I would have headed for California," Quince replied. "I'm not going anywhere until I've cleared my name."

"I hope you can do it, kid. I really do." Jordan was quiet for a moment, then he said, "What do you think, Quince? Do you think Tombs will figure out where we are?"

Quince nodded. "He's bound to. I figure he backtracked when we didn't show up as expected. By now he knows we came over here. We avoided the ambush and we bought some time, but they are going to find us, and they are going to hit us sometime before we make it to Antelope Springs."

"If he does hit us, it should be a very interesting experience," Will said.

"Interesting? That's an odd way of putting it."

Jordan shrugged. "Think about it," he said. "We've got ourselves a regular traveling circus here, wouldn't you say? We have a widow, a spoiled young woman, a sick little girl, a dude gambler, a jackass banker, a crusty old stage driver who is about ready to strangle the banker, a runt of a shotgun guard, and you, an escaped prisoner."

"You left yourself out, Sheriff."

"Ah, yes," Jordan responded, his tone ironic. "Well, I suppose I am the prize package of all. Here I am, a sheriff without jurisdiction, not only harboring but arming an escaped fugitive, and upon my shoulders falls the responsibility of holding it all together."

"I can't think of anyone else better for the job," Quince said.

"Thanks," Jordan replied. He stretched and yawned. "Well, I guess I'll try and grab a few winks." He started to leave then he stopped and turned back toward Quince. "Son, I do hope there is some way we can prove your innocence. Because if we can't, I'll have to take you back."

Quince shook his head. "I really hope it never gets that far, Will, because I'm not going back."

Jordan looked a little surprised. "Are you saying you would fight me, Quince?"

"If need be," Quince confessed with a slight nod.

Jordan smiled thinly and then drew an audible breath. "My friend," he said. "Let us both pray that it never comes to that. Because I wouldn't want to have to kill you."

"Nor I you," Quince replied.

The two men looked at each other for a long moment, then with a slight nod Jordan turned again and started toward the encampment.

Rachel was restlessly shifting on her blanket near the fire when she saw Will Jordan come back into the camp and lie down. Within a few moments the sheriff was snoring contentedly, as were all the others. The young woman envied them, for they had been able to fall asleep so quickly, whereas she was still trying to find a position that was comfortable.

She turned over for what had to be the hundredth time and stared out toward the creekbank. She could make out Quince Fremont standing there, illuminated by the full moon, sometimes looking all around the horizon and other times just staring at the water. She wondered what he was thinking about. More specifically, she wondered if he was thinking about her.

Rachel continued to toss and turn, but no matter how hard she tried, sleep refused to come. Finally she sat up and watched the campfire for a few moments, then she decided to take a little walk. She assumed she would be safe as long as she stayed well within sight and sound of the encampment.

She noiselessly made her way down to the creek, lighted most of the way by the glow of the small campfire, stopping a ways upstream from Quince. Walking to the edge of the stream, she watched the rushing water splashing a brilliant white where it broke over the rocks.

The air caressed her skin like fine silk, carrying on it a hint of woodsmoke and coffee. She suddenly wondered whether anyone was near, and if so, if they would be able to smell the encampment even if they could not see the flames from the fire. Putting the thought from her mind as she pulled her shawl tighter around her shoulders, she looked around as her eyes adjusted to the darkness.

The night sky looked like blue velvet, and the stars glistened like diamonds, while in the distance, barely visible mountain peaks rose in great and mysterious dark slabs against the midnight sky. An owl flew nearby and his wings rustled softly as he passed by.

If Rachel still had any doubts about abandoning her original intention to return to Boston, this night put them to rest. Despite the dangers they were facing, though she could scarcely admit this to herself, perhaps because of them, she had never felt so alive.

Glancing to her right, she saw a large, flat rock, and she walked over and sat. Pulling her knees up under her chin, she stared out at the water, and the constant gurgling of the brook soothed her while she sat in contemplative silence.

She thought back a few hours, when she and Katy O'Leary had sat talking by the fire. The two women had discussed Damon Parker, and Rachel was sure she had detected something in Kate that had not been there earlier in the day. There was a sparkle in her eyes when she spoke of Damon, but when Rachel questioned her about it, Kate insisted it was merely that she was so touched by the gambler's compassion, not something one would expect to find in a person of his profession.

Rachel, on the other hand, was more impressed with Damon's wealth of knowledge about music, literature, and art, subjects she would never have expected a gambler to understand, much less know. She prided herself on her fine Boston education, yet the two of them had wiled away many of the hours during the long journey discussing the works of various artists, writers, and composers. It was clear that the gambler not only knew his subjects well, but held interesting opinions on them. It was also clear to her that Damon Parker's background was not that of the rootless wanderer, and she was very sure that he was much deeper than he appeared to be.

"It's not a good idea for you to wander away from the camp like this," a voice suddenly declared, "though I'll confess I'm glad you did."

Rachel had been so absorbed in her own thoughts that she had neither seen nor heard Quince approach her. Nevertheless she was not surprised by his presence. "Aren't you supposed to be on watch?" she asked.

"I am on watch, which explains why I'm here," Quince said, dryly. "The question is, why are you here?"

"I couldn't sleep."

"You've been traveling hard ever since you left Boston," Quince said. "I can't imagine you not being tired enough to sleep."

"Maybe I just have too much on my mind."

Quince sighed. "I can understand that. I have a lot on my mind, too." His voice softened. "I hope some of it is the same thing."

She still would not look at him. "Quince, what is going to happen to you?"

"What do you mean?"

"As much as I disagree with that awful Mr. Matthews, he is right about one thing. You are an escaped prisoner. When we arrive in Antelope Springs, you will be sent back to prison."

"Yeah, that's what Will Jordan just reminded me," Quince said. "But I'll tell you what I told him. I'm not going back."

"How are you going to arrange that?"

"There is no doubt in my mind that Deekus Tombs is going to attack the stagecoach somewhere between here and Antelope Springs. The money we are carrying is as much bait to him as cheese is to a rat. And when he takes the bait, I'm going to take that two-legged rat."

"I see. So your entire plan is based upon capturing Deekus Tombs and somehow forcing him to clear you. Is that it?"

"That's it," Quince agreed.

"What if it doesn't work out that way?" Rachel asked. "What if you aren't able to capture him?"

"Then I'll figure out some other way. But no matter what happens, I am not going back to prison."

"Even if it means running from the law for the rest of your life?"

"Yes," Quince said. "If it comes to that, I'm prepared to do it."

"That certainly wouldn't be much of a life," Rachel suggested.

"No, it wouldn't be." Quince reached down and put his hand under her chin then gently turned her face up to look into his own. "That's why I could never ask you to come with me. Before a man would ask a woman to marry him, he should have something to offer her . . . a home, security, a future."

Rachel felt her face coloring. "Marriage?" she asked, the word catching in her throat.

"Is the idea so offensive to you?"

"I . . . I don't . . ." Rachel stammered. She was going to tell him that to even talk about such a thing now was inappropriate, but before she could say anything further, Quince lifted her to her feet and kissed her.

Despite her resolve not to get involved with a wanted fugitive, Rachel found herself returning his kiss.

"Damn!" Quince said, breaking off the kiss.

Rachel gasped in surprise. "I kiss you back and that's the way you react?"

"No, it's not that," Quince said quickly. "It's just that . . . well, I told you, I thought about this very thing while I was in prison, and now, here you are, in my arms, and there's nothing I can do about it."

"Oh, but there is," Rachel replied. "We can prove your innocence."

Quince pulled Rachel to him in a big bear hug. "That's all I wanted to hear," he said. "Rachel, girl, I'm going to get Deekus Tombs and make him tell what actually happened that day.

If I have to soak my pants in kerosene and ride down to hell to kick the devil in the backside to do it, it's going to be done."

Rachel laughed. "Well, Quince Fremont, if you insist on doing that, the least I can do is hold the kerosene can for you."

"That's a deal!" Quince said happily.

"The trail goes that way," Deekus Tombs insisted, pointing toward the mountains.

"No it don't. It goes that way, through the pass," Clint Prescott insisted.

"Dammit, I once held up a mule train over here. I know where the trail is."

"Were they pack mules, or were they pullin' a wagon?" Hawk asked.

"They was pack mules," Deekus said.

"Well, there you go, then," Prescott said. "Pack mules can use a mountain trail. A wagon needs a road . . . and the road goes through that pass."

"The moon's gone down, and it's too dark to make out much from sign," Jim Silver said. "Maybe we ought to wait until light and then get a bead on them. I mean, if we strike out down one of those two trails you're arguin' about, and we choose the wrong one, we might lose them."

"All right, all right," Deekus agreed reluctantly. "We'll stay here until dawn." He pulled off a plug of chewing tobacco and stuck it in his cheek. Scowling, he grumbled, "We're supposed to have a friend on the coach. Why in hell don't we get some kind of a signal?"

Beans poked at the dying fire with a long stick until the coals that had been glowing broke out into flames. Then he tossed a few more chunks of wood onto the fire, and when he was satisfied that they had caught, he sat down on a rock and watched them burn.

His gaze fell on Ethan Matthews some thirty feet away from him. The clerk lay sleeping with his arms wrapped securely around the black bag he had carried ever since he had boarded the coach in Rock Creek. And in that bag was one hundred thousand dollars.

Beans tried to imagine what so much money looked like . . . and how long it would take to spend it. The most money he had ever had at one time was $630 . . . the money he had stolen from a Kansas Stage Line.

He hadn't actually stolen it, but he had been a party to the robbery. As a shotgun guard for the Kansas Stage Line, he had inside information as to when a large sum of money was being shipped. He provided the information to some outlaws, then cooperated with them when they held up the stage.

He lost most of the money in a high-stakes

poker game just two days later. The rest he spent on women, whiskey, and food. He remembered that he had eaten a lobster. He had never even seen a lobster before, and it was the best thing he had ever eaten, and he told anyone who cared to listen about that experience. If it was the last thing he did before he died, he was going to eat another lobster.

Thinking about the money in Matthews's satchel, Beans smiled again. With that much money, even with just a share of it, he could leave the territory and maybe go out to San Francisco, or even back East. The law would never think of looking for him back East.

He had heard the Kincaid girl talk about what a wonderful place Boston was, and he wondered how many restaurants Boston had, and how long it would take someone to eat his way through all of them. For certain, the Boston restaurants would have lobster.

Will Jordan wasn't sure what caused him to wake up, but he abruptly opened his eyes and laid there for a moment, feeling as if something was wrong. Glancing over toward the stagecoach, he saw that everything appeared to be all right as it stood clearly illuminated by the bright orange flames from the campfire.

Suddenly he realized what was wrong! He wouldn't be seeing the coach so distinctly unless the campfire was too big. Leaping to his feet, he saw that the fire was blazing brightly, providing a beacon that could lead anyone—including Deekus Tombs and his men—right into camp.

"What the hell!" Jordan bellowed. "Who's on watch here? Who built this fire?"

Quince sat up and rubbed his eyes. "Beans relieved me," he said.

Beans had been sound asleep, slumped forward against a log, but the sudden shout woke him.

"Get that fire down!" Jordan ordered, as he rushed over to contain the blaze.

Beans leapt up and began kicking dirt onto the flames as well. Finally the fire was brought under control and again it became a small glow rather than a huge blaze."

"Beans, what the hell were you trying to do? Send a signal to the outlaws?"

"I'm sorry, Sheriff, I'm sorry!" Beans said. "I guess I just fell asleep and let the fire get away from me."

"Look at the wood on that fire," Quince said. "It didn't just get away. It was built up."

"I put a little wood on the fire, yes, but I didn't think I put all that much."

"That's your problem, Beans, you don't think," Jordan said angrily.

By now everyone was awake, and Jordan turned his attention away from Beans to address the others. "All right, folks, as long as we're all up, we may as well break camp. It'll be light soon and we need to get underway. Especially if anyone happened to see our fire," he added, with yet another glare toward Beans.

Everyone began stirring, rolling up blankets, and packing away cooking gear. The women walked down to the stream and splashed water on their faces and then combed their hair.

When they got back to the others, Kate saw that Damon was squatting down beside Lucy. "How did she take the night?" he asked, as Kate approached.

"Not well," Kate replied. "I think her fever is up. And she seems to be in even more pain than she was before."

"I was afraid of that," Damon said.

Damon stood then, and as the others busied themselves with loading everything back onto the stage coach, the gambler took a bucket and walked down to the stream. There, he broke off chunks of ice that had formed along the edges of the bank, and filled the bucket with it. By the time he returned to the stage, the team was hitched and the passengers were boarding.

As the coach got underway, Damon took out his pocketknife and cut a bit of canvas from the window curtain and then began wrapping it around a large chunk of ice. Quince looked at him as if he had lost his mind.

"Damon, what are you doing?" Quince asked.

"I'm making an ice pack," Damon explained. When he was finished, he handed it to Kate. "Now, Kate, if you would, hold it against her bare skin, right about here," he said, pointing to the lower right side of the girl's abdomen.

Kate looked at him with an expression of bewilderment on her face. "That seems like a strange thing to do," she said. "Lucy is in enough discomfort as it is. Wouldn't this just add to it?"

"No," Damon said. "The ice will serve to numb her stomach so the pain won't be as severe. It will also slow the infection."

"Infection? What infection? She doesn't have a cut of any kind."

Damon sighed. "I haven't told you before, because I didn't want to alarm you. But now I feel I must tell you. Lucy has appendicitis."

"Appendi . . . what?" Kate replied.

"Appendicitis. That means the appendix is swollen and inflamed. I'm hoping that the cold will keep it from bursting before we reach Antelope Springs, but if it does burst, the cold might help retard the spread of infection until your Dr. Presnell can perform an appendectomy . . . that is, remove the appendix. It's a surgical procedure."

"Oh, my God!" Kate exclaimed, putting her hand to her mouth in fright. "That'll be very dangerous, won't it?"

"There is a degree of risk, yes, but it isn't nearly as dangerous as letting the appendix rupture," Damon said. "Go ahead, put the ice pack on her."

Kate put the ice pack on Lucy's stomach, but Lucy instantly cried out in pain. "Oh, Mama, don't! That's so cold it hurts!"

Kate jerked her hand away, but Damon reached across the space between the seats and put his hand on her wrists. Gently, but firmly, he guided the ice pack back to Lucy's stomach. "Keep it there," he ordered. "It will be uncomfortable only briefly, then she won't feel the cold anymore . . . nor, hopefully, the pain."

"All right," Kate agreed, though her expression clearly showed her uncertainty. She held the ice pack in place, despite the whimpers and complaints of the little girl.

"Madam, for the life of me, I can't understand why you insist upon doing everything this man tells you," Ethan Matthews said.

"Well, I think she should listen to him," Quince put in. "I don't know anything about doctoring, but it seems to me like most of it is just common sense. And I've never known anybody with any more common sense than this man. You saw how he managed to get us down the mountain last night."

"Yes, I saw it. It was a damn fool stunt that could've gotten us killed," Matthews sputtered.

"It was a very smart feat," Quince corrected. "I wouldn't call it a stunt at all."

There were murmurs of agreement from the other passengers. Then Damon looked directly into Kate's eyes. "I don't want to force you to do something you don't want to do," he said.

"Nonsense, I trust you," Kate replied.

I trust you! The words were like a dagger, for they were the same words Deborah had said to him just before he operated on her . . . just before he killed her.

For a moment, Damon almost told Kate to take the ice pack away. After all, who was he to give advice? He had walked away from the responsibility of his Hippocratic oath. He was no longer a doctor . . . not in the eyes of the world and certainly not in his own eyes. But just before he said something, Lucy spoke.

"Mr. Parker was right, Mama," she said. "I don't feel the cold anymore, and my stomach's quit hurting."

"There, that's excellent," Damon said, sighing with relief that the numbing had taken effect so quickly.

Chapter Seventeen

The stagecoach had been traveling for about an hour as Quince stared more intently out the window. Something had caught the corner of his eye and as he looked, he saw it again. It was a patch of reflected light, playing along the rocks. Puzzled, he leaned out the window and looked up, then saw that it was Beans's shotgun, flashing in the sun.

"Hold it! Hold it!" he shouted.

"Whoa!" Gib Crabtree called to the team, and with a squeak of brakes, the coach came to a halt.

Quince threw open the door and leapt out, standing with his hands on his hips, staring up at the box.

"What is it?" Jordan asked from his position atop the stage. "Why did you stop us?"

"It's Beans's shotgun," Quince said. "Look over there on the rocks."

Will, Gib, and Beans looked in the direction

that Quince had indicated. The shotgun guard jiggled the weapon, and the little patch of light danced about on the rocks.

"Dammit, Beans! What the hell are you doing?" Gib asked.

"Get that down out of the sun, Beans," Jordan ordered. "The way that thing is flashing, someone could see us for twenty miles."

"I'm sorry!" Beans said, wrapping the barrel in his duster. "It won't happen again. I'll be very careful," he promised.

"It better not happen again," Jordan said with a growl. "First there was the fire, then this. What's next, smoke signals?"

They got back on the road with Quince keeping a sharp eye peeled through the window. Not ten minutes passed when a rifleshot abruptly rang out, followed by the whine of bullets.

"Quince!" Jordan shouted from atop the coach. "They're here! They're behind us!"

"Move over, Will, I'm coming up top!" Quince shouted back. As he threw open the door, he looked at the other passengers and instructed, "Tombs and his men will be shooting high . . . at us. Damon, put the girl and the women on the floor, and you and Matthews lie down on the seats."

"I can shoot as well, you know," Damon yelled over the gunshots coming from up top.

"Are you any good?"

"Not very," Damon admitted.

Quince shook his head. "Then don't do it. If they see that shooting is coming from down in the coach, they'll shoot back and one of you could be hit. Better let us do all the shooting."

"Whatever you say," Damon acquiesced.

Reaching for the luggage rack, Quince pulled himself up on top of the stage. By now, Gib had whipped the horses into a dead run, and the coach was bouncing and lurching at full speed along the little-used wagon road. Beans had left his place in the driver's box and positioned himself on the coach top with the sheriff. Joining the other two, who were lying as flat as they could on top of the stage, Quince began shooting back at the attackers.

A bullet whizzed by his ear.

"How many are there?" he asked.

"I've seen four," Jordan replied.

The wheels of the coach were throwing up a large rooster tail of dust. The dust cloud made it difficult to see clearly enough to get a good shot. But it also provided a screen that made it just as difficult for Deekus Tombs and his men.

Quince got to his knees to take aim when, suddenly the coach hit a deep wagon rut, and he was thrown off balance. He found himself hanging upside down, by his legs, over the side of the coach, his face precariously close to the wheel. Grabbing desperately for something to hold on to, his hand found the side lantern, and he gripped with all his might while dust and rocks were being thrown up into his face.

"Hang on, Quince!" Jordan shouted.

While Beans kept up the shooting, the sheriff hurried to Quince's aid. Quince felt himself being lifted up by the seat of his pants and hauled to safety.

Repositioning themselves, Quince and Jordan resumed firing. Jordan got off a good shot, and Quince saw one of Deekus's men grab his right knee as blood poured through his pant leg.

Deekus threw up his arm. "Fall back, fall back!" he shouted, and the robbers reined in their horses while the coach continued on at full speed.

"We did it!" Jordan shouted triumphantly. "We beat them off!"

"Yeah, but for how long?" Quince asked.

"Dammit, Deekus, they're getting away!" Silver yelled.

"Yeah, and with our money," Hawk Peters added.

"Just hold on, boys," Deekus said. "We wasn't getting anywhere that way." He looked over at Prescott. Prescott was white as a sheet from the pain of his shattered kneecap, and his right leg was covered with blood from the knee down. "There's too many of them bastards for us to take on this way. Who would've thought they would have so many guns?"

"Well, you ain't just gonna let the money get away, are you?" Hawk asked.

"No," Deekus replied, a slow smile working its way over his hard face. "Don't forget, we got us a friend on that coach. I figure if we'll just hang back a bit, he'll get it stopped for us." He chuckled, adding, "Why work so hard when we don't have to?"

"Gib! Hold it up, Gib!" Jordan shouted to the driver. "Deekus and his bunch have pulled back. You can stop the team now."

Looking back over his shoulder, Gib Crabtree satisfied himself that the outlaws were no longer chasing him. "Whoa, horses!" he yelled, hauling back on the reins and pushing the brake lever forward with his foot. The stage squeaked and rattled to a halt, sitting on the lumber road, surrounded by the cloud of dirt and dust that had been thrown up by the gallop. Completely exhausted by their effort, their bodies covered with foam and swat, the horses stood shuddering in their harnesses, their chests heaving and breathing loudly.

"My God, listen to those poor critters," Gib declared in a pained voice. His weathered face wore a worried look. "Damn me if it doesn't just kill my soul to do this to them." Then he smiled. "Weren't they magnificent, though? They gave us all they had, and this after they'd pulled us for two days before I put them to running. But they're plumb wore out now. If I don't give them a rest, they're goin' to drop dead in their tracks, every last one of them."

"Go ahead and give them a rest," Jordan said, shifting around on top of the stagecoach so that he was facing forward. "I think we sort of surprised ol' Deekus there. I don't think we'll be seeing him anymore. He just learned what it's going to cost him to get the money."

"I wouldn't be giving up on him just yet, Will," Quince cautioned, wiping a forearm across his thick sandy hair to keep the sweat from running down into his eyes. "Maybe he won't hit us head-on, but you'd be making a big mistake if you believe he's given up. I can't see Deekus Tombs just walking away from all this money without making another try."

"Well, don't worry, I'm not going to let my guard down, if that's what you mean. But we hurt one of them pretty bad, so he realizes it's not going to be a cinch. I figure he's going to have to lick his wounds for a bit before he makes his next step. He needs this time as much as we need to let our horses blow."

"I'll admit that we probably bought ourselves a little time," Quince agreed. "You might even say we won this battle, as long as we realize that the war isn't over." He lay his rifle down. "If you don't mind, Sheriff, I'm going to hop down and have a look at the folks inside the coach. Deekus and his boys threw a lot of lead at us. I want to make certain no one got hit by a stray bullet."

"Yeah, that's a good idea," Jordan agreed.

Quince dropped down to the ground, then opened the door to the coach and looked inside.

"Any bullets come through here?" he asked, looking directly at Rachel.

"No bullets, just lots of dirt," Rachel replied, rubbing her hands over her face.

Quince chuckled. "Yeah," he said. "I can see that."

The passengers in the coach looked as if they had all been wallowing like hogs, for they were coated with the same thin gray-brown film that now covered the stage, from all the dirt and dust that had been thrown up by the hooves and wheels during the mad dash just completed. Ethan Matthews, drawn up in the front left corner of the coach, was clutching a handkerchief to his nose.

"I guess it got a little rough for you folks, but we couldn't help it. Is everybody all right?" Quince asked.

"No, we are not all right!" Matthews replied testily, his fingers smoothing his small, closely clipped, dirt-caked mustache. "That fool driver nearly broke our necks with that wild ride he just gave us!"

"You're still alive, aren't you, mister?" Quince snapped.

"Barely."

"Well, barely's better'n dead. You should be thankful. Believe me, you wouldn't even be that if Deekus had caught up with us."

"I disagree. In fact, I think we should stop and wait for Tombs to come to us," Matthews said.

"What? You think we should stop and wait for him? What's the matter with you, mister? Are you crazy?"

"On the contrary, sir. I consider myself to be the only sane person here. Perhaps if we stopped the coach and approached Mr. Tombs under a flag of truce, we could negotiate with him."

"Negotiate? Negotiate for what?"

"Why, we would negotiate for our lives, of course," Matthews said. "I have some degree of experience in business negotiations. I'm a banker, after all. I would be more than glad to represent our side in this matter. I know that the only thing Tombs wants is the money. If we simply give it to him, I'm sure he would ride away and leave us alone. I don't believe he would kill us without any reason."

"Those men we buried back at the Belle

Fourche way station might disagree with you, Mr. Matthews," Quince said. "And anyway, you're the one carrying the money, so that means you're the one Deekus Tombs and his men are after. I would think you'd appreciate our fighting them off more than anyone."

"Yes, well, whereas I am carrying the money, it is, after all, the Rock Creek Bank's money and not my own," Matthews said.

Quince ran an impatient hand through his dust-streaked hair. "It may be the bank's money, but you do have some responsibility toward it, do you not?"

"I have some responsibility, of course, but I think we have made an adequate attempt to defend it," the little banker countered. "We have fought well, and there would be no dishonor now in surrendering to the demands of Deekus Tombs. I know of no code of honor that would require us to die for someone else's money."

"No, Mr. Matthews, I don't suppose you would know of such a code of honor," Quince said. "But then, what difference would it make if you did know of one? I'm not sure someone like you would abide by any such rules, anyway."

"Sir! Are you, a prison escapee, accusing me, a respected banker, of being dishonest?"

"No, just a man without honor," Quince said.

"And in my book, you can't have one without the other."

Dismissing the unpleasant Ethan Matthews, Quince looked over at Kate O'Leary. Kate was holding Lucy's head on her lap. Rachel was holding the girl's feet, while Damon was kneeling between the seats, with his hand resting on Lucy's stomach.

"The sheriff wants to know how the little girl is doing," Quince said. "And I'd like to know myself."

Studying Lucy, Quince was not at all reassured by the child's appearance. Her face was very pale, and it was obvious that she was hurting badly.

"The ride we just took didn't help things much," Damon said.

"I'm sorry about the ride, there was nothing we could—"

Damon held up his hand, cutting off Quince's apology. "No, no, don't start apologizing. I know it couldn't be helped. I was just making an observation, is all. I wasn't complaining."

It wasn't until then that Quince realized that Damon had lifted the young girl's dress up far enough to allow him to look at her bare stomach. Damon finished his examination, then pulled the dress back down.

"How is she?" the girl's mother asked anxiously.

"There's no doubt that she is in a great deal

of discomfort," Damon replied. Then he smiled. "However, from everything I can determine, any pain she's feeling now is from the banging around of the rough ride. I'm almost positive that her appendix hasn't burst."

"Good," Kate breathed. Then she tilted her head and stared intently at Damon. "I mean, I think that's good, isn't it?"

"Oh, yes, it's good." Damon reached down into the bucket and pulled out another chunk of ice. "I sure wish we had some more ice, though," he said, as he wrapped another chunk in canvas. "I'm afraid this is our last piece." He handed it across to Kate.

Just then Will Jordan climbed down from the top of the coach and stood beside Quince, looking in through the doorway.

"No damages in here," Quince reported.

"Good," the sheriff declared. "Come on, son, let's hike back along the road a piece and see if we can get an idea as to where Deekus Tombs might be."

"All right," Quince agreed, and the two men started walking.

"How's the little girl doing?" Jordan asked.

"Well, according to Damon, whatever it is that's ailing her hasn't burst, whatever that means. And that's supposed to be a good sign," Quince answered. "But she's in a lot of pain."

"Poor kid," Jordan said, sighing. "I wish we

could just give her a nice, smooth ride on in to the doctor." The sheriff's eyes turned cold. "It really makes me furious that Tombs put that child through all this."

"Deekus Tombs has never been mistaken for a man of compassion," Quince said.

When they were far enough away from the coach to ensure that they couldn't be overheard, the lawman and his prisoner turned and looked back toward the others. Gib was up at the front of the team, examining his horses, and Beans was leaning nonchalantly against the side of the coach, cradling his shotgun in his arms. Matthews was the only passenger who had left the coach, and he was walking around nervously, stretching his legs.

Looking back at Quince, Jordan said, "I want to talk to you about Beans."

"What about him?"

"Turns out he served some time in a Kansas prison. And it was for robbing a coach. To be more specific, it was for being the inside man and setting up the robbery."

"How do you know this?"

"Soon after he started working for the Wyoming Coach and Express Company, I found an old wanted poster on him," Jordan explained. "So I checked up on him. I learned that he wasn't wanted anymore, as he had served his time and been given a full release."

"I see. Did you tell the Wyoming Express people?"

"No," Jordan replied, shaking his head. "I know, I know, I probably should have. But I sort of like Beans, cantankerous old sort that he is, and I figured he had already paid society whatever debt he owed. If he was trying to make an honest living now, I didn't want to do anything that would cause him problems. Besides, I figure since the stagecoach company never asked anything about him, it wasn't my place to volunteer any information."

Bending down, Quince picked up a rock and started tossing it from hand to hand. "How has he worked out?"

"Pretty well, from all I hear. Beans has been one of their best employees . . . at least, he has been 'till now."

"Until now?"

"Quince, do you think it's possible that Beans may be in cahoots with Tombs?"

"Do you?"

"Well, there was the business with the fire last night. You know, he was the one on watch when it flared up like it did. It was so bright that Tombs had to have seen it. Then there was the shotgun flashing in the sun. He may as well have been signaling with a mirror. And it was right afterward that Tombs attacked us."

"Could just be coincidence."

"I suppose it could be," Jordan answered. "But I also know that just before we left Rock Creek, Beans sent a telegram. In fact, the stagecoach was almost late leaving because of it."

"You think he sent a telegram to Deekus Tombs, telling about the money?"

"He could have."

"How? Where would Tombs get such a message?"

"I don't know. Maybe they had something worked out."

"I don't know," Quince said. "I'm like you, I'm sort of partial to ol' Beans. But since you are already suspicious, I figure I'd better give you one more piece of information about him."

"What's that?"

"He and Deekus Tombs were cellmates."

"What? How do you know that?"

"He told me," Quince replied.

"Then that cinches it," Jordan said.

Quince shook his head. "Not necessarily."

"Why not?"

"Well, Beans himself is the one who told me. If he really was in on this, do you think he would tell me about being in prison with Tombs if he was in on this?"

"I don't know. Maybe he told you because you are a fellow convict and he was trying to impress you."

"Could be," Quince admitted.

Jordan looked hard at Quince. "I'm sorry, Quince, but I've got to ask this. If Beans is in on this, and he offered you part of the money to keep quiet, you would let me know, wouldn't you?"

Scowling, Quince threw the rock hard against a tree. Then he turned to the sheriff. "I thought you knew me better than to ask a question like that. Are you saying that you aren't completely convinced that my brother and I were innocent?"

"Oh, I don't have the slightest doubt that you were innocent of the charge that sent you to prison," Jordan said. "But you have been serving time for it, after all, and it is only human nature to want to get even. You may figure you're owed some of the money that's on this stage."

"If you really believe that, Will, why are you letting me carry a gun?"

"I don't know. Because I *don't* believe it, I guess," Jordan admitted. "Hell, I'm not supposed to be on this stage anyway. If my horse hadn't gone lame, I would already be back in Antelope Springs, wondering what's taking the stage so long."

Quince smiled. "Well, then, aren't you glad you're here with us so your curiosity can be satisfied?"

Laughing, the lawman replied, "You know

what they say, Quince. Curiosity once killed a cat. I just hope it doesn't hold true for sheriffs."

"Sheriff, Quince," Gib Crabtree called. "The horses have their wind back. I think we can leave."

Jordan and Quince returned to the coach and everyone boarded, with Jordan and Quince once again riding on top, their weapons held at the ready.

Chapter Eighteen

The coach got no farther than half a mile when they felt a lurch and a shudder.

"Whoa!" Gib called to his team, hauling back on the reins again.

"What is it?" Jordan asked. "What happened?"

"If it's not one thing, it's another," Gib muttered, tying off the reins. "Somethin's wrong with one of the wheels. One of the ones in the rear, I think. Feels like it's locked up tighter'n a drum."

Gib climbed down from the coach, while everyone watched with concern. Checking the wheels, he found the troublesome one and put his hand on the hub. He then removed some of the axle grease and rubbed it between his fingers.

"I'll be damned," he said.

"What is it?" Jordan called from atop the coach.

Holding his grease-stained fingers up toward the lawman, Gib answered. "This is full of grit.

Someone has packed dirt in the hub." Narrowing his eyes, he added, "Somebody on this here stage don't want us to get through."

"But who would do such a thing?" Rachel asked.

"I'll tell you who it is," Ethan Matthews said, climbing out of the stage and brushing himself off. "It's him!" He pointed an accusing finger up at Quince. "I warned all of you! I told you not to let that outlaw ride with us! Now look what he has done!"

"We don't know that he did it," Jordan said.

"Well, I know he did it, whether any of the rest of you want to admit it or not!" the banker declared in a self-righteous voice.

"Right now, it don't make no difference who done it," Gib grumbled. "The thing we gotta do is get that wheel off and get all the dirty grease out of there. Then I can goop her down good with some clean grease, and we can reset the wheel and get going."

"How long is all that going to take?" Damon asked, sticking his head out the window.

"Not too long, if we'll just get on it," the driver answered.

Pointing up to a shadowed, snow-covered ledge some fifty feet up the side of the mountain that bordered the road, Damon said, "I've run out of ice for the little girl's stomach. Will I have time to climb up there and get some snow?"

Gib looked up at the snowbank then nodded. "Sure," he said. "I reckon you'll have time to do that."

"Good." Damon smiled at Kate. "Don't worry, we'll keep her comfortable."

"Thank you, Damon," Kate replied.

After Damon stepped down from the coach, Gib stuck his head inside. "Ma'am, I'm sorry, but you an' the little girl are going to have to get out, too. It can't be helped."

"Of course, I understand," Kate replied. She helped Lucy out of the coach, and they walked over to the side of the road, then sat down.

"It's going to take three of us to get this stage lifted. Sheriff, if you and Quince will help Beans get the coach raised up, I'll slide the jack under the axle. Then I can pull the wheel." He smiled, ruefully. "I'm afraid this here jack don't do nothin' to make our job any easier. All it does is provide a base to rest the axle on once we get 'er raised."

"I hope you don't expect me to help," Matthews said.

"I wouldn't dream of asking you to get your hands dirty, Mr. Matthews," Gib said with a snort. "But if it isn't too much trouble, you might help the women keep an eye open for Deekus Tombs and his bunch."

Kate found a place for Lucy, then with the little girl out of the way, she joined Rachel and

Matthews, each of them taking up posts to act as lookouts.

The men began working. It proved to be hard, heavy labor, and they were well into it, sweating and shoving to make sure the coach was lifted and the jack put in position.

Suddenly Lucy called out, "Mama, I'm hurting real bad!"

Kate's head whipped around toward her daughter, then she looked back at Rachel and Matthews. "I have to go to her," she said.

"Of course you do," Rachel agreed.

Rachel watched Kate hurry toward the child. In an uncharacteristic show of concern, Matthews said, "Miss Kincaid, if you want to go help your friend, I'll keep watch."

"Thank you, Mr. Matthews. I appreciate that." Rachel hurried over to see what assistance she could provide.

For the next few minutes, all were involved in what they were doing. The women were trying to soothe Lucy, while the four men grunted and groaned as they worked on the coach wheel.

Suddenly an evil laugh rang out and a loud, gruff voice taunted, "Well, now, lookee here, would you?"

Everyone turned to see Deekus Tombs and two other men pointing their pistols at them.

"Tombs!" Quince growled.

"What are you doing here, Fremont? If you had any sense, you'd be in California by now."

"I'm not going anywhere until you clear my name."

"Until *I* clear it? How am I supposed to do that? You expect me to go into court?"

"I would appreciate it," Quince said dryly.

Tombs laughed out loud. "That's funny, Fremont. That's really funny. Too bad you don't *really* ride with me. You'd be worth a few laughs."

"Then you are admitting that he and his brother were set-up?" Jordan asked.

"Yeah, sure, I'll admit it," Tombs said. "For all the good it'll do him."

All the while Tombs was talking, Beans was edging ever closer to his shotgun. Tombs turned his pistol toward Beans, and shook his head. "Try it, Beans, and you are a dead man," he said.

Beans jerked back.

"Instead of just leavin' that scar on your face, I shoulda slit your throat back there in prison when I had the chance. You sure did cause me a peck of trouble by rattin' on me."

"You didn't have to kill that kid in the pen, Deekus. All he was doin' was tryin' to protect what was rightly his."

Deekus scoffed. "In prison things belong to whoever is strong enough to take it. No matter

what that kid had, it was mine for the taking."
He made motion with his pistol. "Now, back
away from that scattergun."

Beans did as he was instructed.

"That's more like it."

"Did you bring a horse for me?" Matthews
asked.

"You asked me to, didn't you?" Tombs replied. "When have I ever not done what you
asked?"

"What?" Jordan gasped. "Matthews . . . you
mean you are in cahoots with this polecat?"

"I don't appreciate you calling my brother a
polecat," Matthews said. There was a precipi-
tous change in Matthews's demeanor. No longer
the whining, sniveling banker, he was crisp and
sure of himself.

"Your brother? You mean your name isn't
Matthews?"

"His name is Matthews and so is mine," Deekus said. He laughed. "I just call myself Tombs,
'cause I've put so many men in the grave."

"Where's Prescott?" Matthews asked.

Tombs motioned toward Quince, Jordan, and
Beans. "One of these three killed him."

"You mean he's dead?"

"He wasn't when we left him, but he's most
likely dead now," Deekus said. "He got his
kneecap shot off and we had to leave him back
along the trail."

"You mean you just left one of your own men to die?" Gib asked.

"We all take our chances in this business. Anyway, what are you concerned for? You're the ones that shot him, not me," Tombs said.

"Ahh, Mr. Parker, do come join us, won't you?" Matthews called.

Because Damon had been collecting snow, he had not been noticed by the outlaws when they arrived. Taking advantage of that, Damon began slipping down the side of the mountain with his gun drawn. He had made no attempt to conceal his approach from Matthews, because he still thought Matthews was one of their own.

When Tombs saw the little derringer Damon was carrying, he laughed out loud. "Now, just what the hell did you plan to do with that pop gun?" he asked. He made a motion with his own pistol. "Get over there with the others."

"Sorry, gentlemen," Damon said as he joined Quince, Jordan, Gib, and Beans. "I didn't realize the little pipsqueak was one of them."

Tombs turned to Hawk Peters and Jim Silver. "You two men go back and bring up the horses. Ethan and I will take care of business here."

Tombs waited until the two men were gone, then he turned toward Matthews. "It's your call, big brother. What do we do with them?"

"We're going to have to kill them," Matthews

said matter-of-factly. "We can't afford to leave any witnesses."

"Matthews, you don't mean you are going to kill the women, too?" Damon asked in a horror-stricken voice.

"If we kill all of you, they won't survive out here," Matthews said. "Believe me, this is much more humane than just letting them die."

"Oh, yes, you are quite the humanitarian," Damon said with a sneer.

"Wait a minute," Matthews suddenly said. "Where is the Kincaid woman?"

"What?" Tombs asked.

Matthews pointed toward Kate and her daughter. "The other woman is missing."

"I'm not missing," a woman's voice called from behind the coach. "I'm right here."

Both Tombs and Matthews turned toward the coach, then gasped out loud. Rachel was standing behind them wearing nothing but a smile. The impact of her total nudity shocked the two men into momentary insensibility and they stood there with their mouths wide open. Without realizing what he was doing, Deekus Tombs lowered his pistol.

That was the opportunity Quince was looking for, and while Tombs and Matthews were distracted, he drew his own pistol.

"Tombs!" he called.

Realizing then that he had been tricked, Tombs whirled around, firing as he did so. His shot went wild, but Quince's bullet found its mark. Tombs went down hard.

At that moment, Peters and Silver were returning with the horses. Seeing what was happening, they drew their own pistols but, by now, Jordan, Gib, and Beans had their guns back as well. The firefight was brief and intense and when the last echo faded away, Deekus Tombs, Hawk Peters, and Jim Silver lay dead. Ethan Matthews had returned to the whimpering lout they had known before, as he stood before them with his arms raised, begging not to be shot.

"Give me one good reason why I shouldn't kill you," Quince growled.

"Because I'm the only one left who can clear your name," Matthews answered.

"Quince, that sounds like reason enough," Jordan said. "And with all of us as witnesses, he can't go back on it now."

"Yes. In the meantime, I suggest we get that wheel back on and get to Antelope Springs as quickly as we can," Damon said. "We still have a sick little girl on our hands."

As soon as the wheel was remounted, everyone reboarded the coach. The handcuffs that Jordan had used on Quince at the beginning of the trip were now on Matthews, as he was put on top of the coach and cuffed to the luggage rail.

Just as Jordan was about to step into the coach, he looked up at Beans. "Beans, I owe you an apology," he said.

"You thought I was with Tombs?"

"Yeah," the sheriff admitted.

"Why? Because I was in prison once?"

"Partly," Jordan admitted. "But also because I saw you go into the telegraph office back in Rock Creek just before we left. I thought maybe you had sent some sort of message to Tombs. Now, I know it's none of my business to ask, but just who did you send a telegram to?"

"Why, I sent it to Mr. Kincaid."

"Kincaid? You mean Rachel's pa? Why did you send a telegram to him?"

"Because he give me two dollars to let him know that his daughter had got in on the train okay, and would be on the stage, comin' home."

Smiling sheepishly, the lawman said, "I reckon I could've saved myself a lot of trouble if I had just asked."

Beans smiled back at him. "Yeah, I reckon you could've."

Chapter Nineteen

It was evident that Lucy's condition was steadily worsening. Her pain had increased, her fever was up, and her pulse rate was rapid and thready. Damon never left the girl's side, keeping a steady watch over her.

He looked up at Kate, whose face was pale with fear, and his heart went out to the beautiful young mother. Putting his hand over hers, he said softly, "She'll make it. I promise."

A tear trickled down Kate's cheek, and her lower lip trembled. "How can you be so sure?" she asked, her voice barely a whisper.

"I just am. Trust me."

"I do trust you," Kate said.

He squeezed her hand affectionately, then turned all his attention back to the little girl.

Whenever the road would allow it, Gib Crabtree kept the horses going at a fast trot. They were coming down from the mountain now, and the road was a great deal better than it had been. As a result, they were able to make much better time than had been possible at any time since leaving the main road.

They rolled into Antelope Springs at twenty minutes before midnight, and Gib didn't even stop at the stage depot. Instead, he urged the team into a gallop, and the coach rumbled down the main street until it reached Dr. Presnell's office.

The coach lurched to a halt, and Damon leapt down and ran to the physician's door. He pounded hard for a few moments and then lights came on inside. Several more moments passed before the door was finally flung open. An elderly man clad in a nightshirt stood in a doorway holding a kerosene lamp.

"Yes? What can I do for you?"

"We have a critically ill child on board the stagecoach, Doctor."

"Get the child inside," Doctor Presnell ordered.

Will Jordan scooped the little girl up and gently carried her inside. Kate came with her, and Dr. Presnell recognized her at once.

"Kate, I'm glad to see you back in Antelope Springs," the doctor said. "We've missed you around here. I'm sorry little Lucy is sick though. What is wrong with her?"

By now, everyone from the coach had crowded inside, but Jordan started back toward the door. "Let me know what happens, will you?" he said to the others. "I've got to get my prisoner in jail."

"Your prisoner?" Rachel asked, anxiously.

Jordan smiled, and nodded toward the coach. "Matthews," he said. "Not Quince."

"Doctor, the girl has appendicitis," Damon said.

"What makes you think the child is suffering from appendicitis?" Dr. Presnell asked.

"She has severe abdominal pain that started near the umbilicus, then localized in the lower right side. She has no appetite and has suffered from nausea and fever. Her pulse has remained strong, but is rapid."

A surprised look washed over Presnell's face. "You're right," he said. "Those *are* the symptoms of appendicitis."

"I stabilized the condition by the application of ice packs. It numbed her against the pain and kept the appendix from rupturing so far, but you're going to have to operate, Doctor. Her appendix must come out."

"Let's not be so hasty."

"No, that's just it, Dr. Presnell. We *must* be hasty. This child has been suffering for days. We have waited as long as we can."

"Mister, I'm not sure you understand what you're saying," the doctor replied. "You're talking about invasive surgery." Presnell shook his head. "I can't do that. Why, the girl could die."

"The chances are greater of her dying if you don't do it," Damon said. "I agree, there is some degree of danger, but it can be greatly minimized if you do the procedure properly."

"And I suppose you are going to tell me how to do it properly?"

"If you wish," Damon said, ignoring the doctor's mocking tone. "Make a transverse incision, then ligate the mesoappendix and remove it by the Paquelin cautery. Tie off the stump and cauterize it, then close her back up. But make certain that your hands and the instruments you use are absolutely clean. You must introduce nothing into the wound that could cause infection."

By now everyone was looking at Damon with expressions of shock on their faces.

"Who are you?" Kate finally asked. "You are obviously not a gambler."

"I am now," he told her.

"And before now?" Kate asked.

Damon let out a long sigh. "I was a doctor," he finally said.

"What is your name?" Presnell asked.

"Parker," Kate answered for him.

"Actually, that is my middle name," Damon said. "My whole name is Damon Parker Kensington."

"Kensington? *You're* Dr. Kensington?"

"Yes."

"Well, I'll be damned. Doctor, the entire world is looking for you."

Looking more confused than ever, Kate remarked, "Dr. Presnell, you mean you have heard of him?"

"Of course I have," Presnell said. "My dear, your friend here was one of the most renowned surgeons in the country. Why, I even read about him out here." Turning to Damon, he asked, "But what happened to you, Dr. Kensington? You just dropped out of sight, as I recall."

"Look," Damon said. "We can discuss this all later. The most important thing now is to operate on the girl. If you don't get that appendix out soon, it's going to rupture. I don't have to tell you that if that happens, the girl will die."

Shaking his head firmly, Presnell declared, "It's not that simple."

"If you wish, I will assist."

Presnell shook his head again. "You don't understand. I simply can't do it. I don't have the skills for such an operation. And even if I did, my hands just wouldn't cooperate." He held up his fingers, and Damon saw that they were twisted and gnarled by arthritis.

"But you must have performed operations," Damon insisted.

"Oh, yes I've set a few bones and extracted

more than my share of bullets. I'm all right as a country doctor, handing out medicine and the like, but I can't handle a scalpel. No, Doctor, if this girl's appendix is going to come out, then *you* are the one who will have to take it out."

The gambler's face turned pale. "Me? No, absolutely not. The girl is your patient, not mine."

"Oh, Damon, you can do the operation, can't you?" Kate asked, wringing her hands and looking up at him pleadingly.

"Kate, you don't know what you are asking of me," Damon said.

"Oh, but I do know," Kate replied. "I'm asking you to save my child."

Damon started to object, but he quickly realized that there was no other option if the girl was to survive. His decision was forced when Lucy clutched her side and cried out in agony. Bending over the girl, Damon examined her and realized that the appendix was on the verge of rupturing.

He stood up, his face tortured. "Dammit!" he whispered. Closing his eyes, he pinched the bridge of his nose for a moment and then took a deep breath and let out a long and slow sigh. "All right," he finally relented. "All right, I'll do the operation."

"I'll assist," Presnell offered. "What instruments will you need?"

Damon told him and then asked, "Do you have any carbolic acid?"

"Yes, I do," the elderly physician replied.

"Would you please pour it into a tray and then empty the surgical instruments into that tray?"

"Yes, of course, Doctor," Presnell replied.

Damon then started preparing Lucy for the operation, washing her thoroughly and then administering chloroform to anesthetize her. He then scrubbed his own hands repeatedly and, with that done, returned to his patient.

Finally, looking up from his young patient, Damon told the others, "I want all of you to wait outside. The fewer people there are around the patient, the less chance there will be of infection."

Kate was clearly reluctant to leave her daughter, but at Rachel's gentle urging that it would be better for Lucy if she did, Kate joined the others.

While Dr. Presnell was scrubbing, Damon stood over the little girl. His heart was beating fast as he held his hands out in front of him, palms up. Though he had done many appendectomies in his career, always considering them simple operations, it had been a long time since he last did one. His confidence had been shattered by his finacée's death. Now this girl and her mother were much more than an impersonal patient and family—just as Deborah had been important to him when he had operated on her tumor against the advice of his fellow surgeons.

He breathed a quick prayer; then, when Presnell joined him at the table and handed him the scalpel, Damon took it in hand and began.

Cutting into the girl's abdomen, he bared the swollen appendix. He worked quickly and efficiently and began making the incisions and slicing through the tissue required to remove the diseased organ.

Suddenly the girl went into respiratory arrest. Damon felt his own heart begin pounding, and he cried, "No! Not again! I won't let this happen again!"

Working desperately, he finally managed to pull Lucy out of the crisis and reestablish a steady heartbeat and respiration. He was sweating profusely, and Dr. Presnell dabbed gauze on the surgeon's forehead, mopping it dry.

"That was close, son," Presnell breathed.

"Too close," Damon agreed.

Minutes later, Damon removed the diseased organ and began closing up the wound. With the last suture finally in place, he sighed with relief and then put the bloodied scalpel back into the tray and walked wearily to the door. He leaned against the doorjamb for a moment, letting his heart slow down, then he opened the door.

Kate, who had been pacing anxiously, stopped short and then rushed to him. "How—?"

"She's going to be just fine," Damon said before she could finish her question. "There is nothing to worry about now."

With a shout of joy, Kate threw herself into Damon's arms.

A week later, Lucy was released from the doctor's clinic, and Kate celebrated with a dinner in her newly reopened hotel. She invited everyone who had been on the stage—except for Ethan Matthews, of course—plus Rachel's mother and father, Gib Crabtree's wife, and, of course, Dr. Presnell.

It was an exceptionally festive dinner. Lucy was healthy again, as evidenced by the return of her appetite, which enabled her to eat two huge pieces of apple pie. Rachel's parents were happy to have her home again, and Quince Fremont was celebrating the fact that he had just received official notification that the original court order that sent him to prison had been reversed. Further, he had received a full pardon from the governor for the prison break.

"I'll suppose you'll be staying on out at your ranch?" asked Rachel's father, Kevin Kincaid.

"I don't have a ranch anymore."

Kincaid cleared his throat. "Sure you do, if you'd be willing to buy it back from me."

"From you?"

"When it was put up for sale for taxes, I bought it," Kincaid explained. "I'll sell it to you for exactly what I paid for it."

"You would do that?" Quince asked, excitedly. Then he stopped. "It doesn't matter. I can't pay you."

"Suppose I loaned you a hundred head of cattle, bulls and cows, to get you started? You can pay me for the land when you can pay me. Are you interested?"

"Well, sure, I'm interested!" Quince exclaimed. "That would be wonderful! I mean, that's much more than I would have ever dreamed could happen. I don't know how I will ever be able to thank you."

Kincaid chuckled. "Young man, consider it the act of a selfish parent. I don't want my daughter going back to Boston, and I figure having you around here just may keep her in Wyoming." He laughed, adding, "I have a feeling from the way you two look at each other it's all going to be in the family, anyway."

Quince's grin grew even broader as he reached over to take Rachel's hand. "Mr. Kincaid, if I have anything to say about it, that's exactly the way it's going to be."

"Well," Dr. Presnell spoke up, "now that that's settled, I wonder if we could prevail upon Dr. Kensington to stay here as well. I could use a young partner . . . and Wyoming could certainly use a good surgeon." He smiled at the younger physician and asked, "What do you say, Damon?"

"I don't know," Damon replied. He turned to Kate and put his hand on hers. "What do you think, Kate? Does Wyoming need me?"

"I don't know about Wyoming," Kate answered, putting her hand over his, her brown eyes sparkling with pleasure. "But I sure do."